DATES
ON MY
FINGERS

DATES
ON MY
FINGERS

MUHSIN AL-RAMLI

Translated by Luke Leafgren

The American University in Cairo Press
Cairo   New York

First published in 2014 by
The American University in Cairo Press
113 Sharia Kasr el Aini, Cairo, Egypt
420 Fifth Avenue, New York, NY 10018
www.aucpress.com

Exclusive distribution outside Egypt and North America by I.B.Tauris & Co Ltd.,
6 Salem Road, London, W2 4BU

Dar el Kutub No. 14526/13
ISBN 978 977 416 644 0

Dar el Kutub Cataloging-in-Publication Data

al-Ramli, Muhsin
          Dates on my fingers/Muhsin al-Ramli; Translated by Luke Leafgren—
    Cairo: The American University in Cairo Press, 2014
          p.   cm.
          ISBN: 978 977 416 644 0
          1. Arabic Fiction
          I. Leafgren, Luke (tr)
          892.73

1 2 3 4 5   18 17 16 15 14

Designed by Jon W. Stoy
Printed in Egypt

To Iraq, the cradle of my childhood
and the cradle of civilization

To Spain, my way station of peace
after a long road crowded with wars

CHAPTER 1

I wouldn't have been able to write my family's story and expose its shame if my father hadn't encouraged me to do so while cutting my hair in his Madrid club. "Write whatever you want," he said. "Nothing will happen worse than has already happened. This world is all fucked up."

At the time, I didn't comment on what he had said, forced as I was to focus on his razor, which nearly took off the skin behind my ear.

The story began on the day that my father, Noah, went with my sister Istabraq to the doctors in the city, seeking treatment for the illness that had made her waste away and ooze yellow diarrhea into her clothes. She kept eating carob powder, which the old wise women had prescribed, but that didn't help at all. Her body became skin and bones, and her breasts drooped down, even though she was only fourteen at the time. She turned a pale yellow, like the leaves of tobacco.

All the same, she seemed more beautiful than the other girls her age in the village because she was kept out of the sun in the fields, which dyed everyone's face the color of old wood. My mother wasn't able to give her any hard work on the farm, so Istabraq was limited to performing small chores in the house, such as making the beds, washing the dishes, sweeping the floors, and hanging out the laundry. Istabraq had been born a twin, but her sister, Sundus, died at nine months. They had been so, so small, squirming in the cradle like two rats drenched in milk. We had all expected Istabraq would die too, but she kept on living. She remained skinny and pale, but she was beautiful and had a good heart.

Noah set off from our first village, Subh, in the afternoon, taking his daughter, who had put perfume on her clothes. They arrived at the city of Tikrit an hour later. On their way to the doctor's office, Istabraq walked a step behind Noah, who was clearing a path for her on the market sidewalk. As a black Mercedes drove past slowly, a hand stretched out from its window to grab Istabraq's butt, and a voice was heard: "Nice ass!"

The young girl cried out in fear, and her father spun around. He immediately grabbed the neck of the driver, shouting furiously in his face, "You son of a bitch!" He lifted him up, as someone might lift a jar by its neck, until he had pulled him out of the car through the window.

The driver was a skinny youth wearing blue sunglasses above his first small mustache. He was dressed in a traditional Arabic robe, white and loose, with a wide leather belt around his waist. A pistol hung down at his side. The empty black car continued its slow course until it collided with a parked car and ground to a halt. Meanwhile, Noah rained blows and curses down upon the young man, who was crying out, "Do you know whose son I am?!"

Without caring and without stopping the savage blows, Noah replied, "Yes, I know: your father was a dog, and your mother a whore!"

The white of the robe was stained with the boy's red blood. He tried to reach for his pistol, but Noah twisted his arm and lifted him upward before smashing him onto the ground. The boy lay still on his face, not moving. Meanwhile, a tide of fury swept Noah away. He bent down and took the revolver from its holster. Opening the chamber, he removed three bullets and threw the pistol into the sewer drain. He pulled away the boy's clothes to reveal his butt and began forcing the bullets into his anus. He pushed in two before he found himself surrounded by the shop owners and the "beasts of burden," as the market's porters were called. The crowd tackled Noah, who was thrashing like a bull. They yelled at him, "Are you crazy? This is the nephew of the vice president's secretary!"

Afterward, Noah found himself being carried from the darkness of a police beating to the darkness of a prison cell. He didn't know anything about Istabraq, who, when she saw the blood, soiled her perfumed dress with yellow diarrhea. She sat down in front of a nearby storefront, crying and shaking like a palm branch in the rain. She remained there until some kind strangers brought her back to Subh Village, where her mother washed her and wrapped her up in bed. Her grandfather, Mutlaq, sat at the head of her bed, and she told him what had happened. Mutlaq leapt up, calling to the family, "If a dog barks at you, don't bark at it; but if it bites you, bite it back!"

That maxim was his philosophy of life, and he had been famous for it throughout the surrounding villages since childhood. At that time, he attended the lessons of Mullah Abd al-Hamid every day, carrying the cloth tote that his mother had made for him by cutting off the bottom half of a bag of rice. She embroidered a winged toddler onto its side and sewed on a strap so he could put it over his shoulder.

3

The tote would hang down under his arm, carrying a copy of the Qur'an, a notebook with gray paper, a round loaf of bread, a handful of dates, and an onion—just like the bags of all the village boys who were learning the Qur'an from Mullah Abd al-Hamid.

One day, on his way to the mosque, a dog blocked his way and barked at him. Mutlaq walked quickly past it, but the dog walked just as quickly after him. Mutlaq ran, and the dog ran in pursuit. Mutlaq stopped to pick up a stone to throw, but the dog jumped up onto his back. Mutlaq twisted around, and the two fell, wrestling on the ground. The dog dug its claws into Mutlaq's neck and bit his leg. In response to Mutlaq's blows, the dog only increased its barking and the ferocity of its attack. Then, at one point in the struggle, Mutlaq found the dog's neck in front of his face, and he bit it so hard that the dog went still and made no other sound than a low, confused whimpering. It scampered away, tail between its legs, without once turning around. Meanwhile, Mutlaq continued on his way to the mosque, limping. When the mullah asked him about the blood and why he was late, Mutlaq responded in the presence of all the other boys, "A dog barked at me; I didn't bark at it. But it bit me, so I bit it back!"

The mullah was silent for a moment. Then he smiled and said, "Give him a round of applause!"

He took off his turban and used it to bandage Mutlaq's leg. Then he gave him a handful of dates and patted him on the shoulder. Since that time, this story about him has been famous, and Mutlaq began to take pride in it, considering his words to be a maxim he had discovered, a maxim sealed by the honor Mullah Abd al-Hamid had shown him: "A thousand mercies upon your soul, O Mullah Abd al-Hamid!"

4

Up leapt Grandfather Mutlaq, who took pride in bearing the name of our first ancestor, which means 'The Absolute.' He summoned his nine sons and all his grandsons, his brothers with their sons and grandsons, and his cousins with their sons and grandsons. He said to them, "Get your weapons and your cars ready for us to storm Tikrit and break Noah out of prison! For if we keep still when they give us the finger, they will mount up and ride us to the ground!"

So everyone hurried to get their clubs, swords, daggers, multi-pronged fishing spears, rifles, and pistols out from behind the headboards and from the garbage dumps where they were buried. My mother pointed to a spot in the mud wall of our house for me to break open once she had taken down the wall hanging of the "Chair Verse" from the Qur'an that was covering it. She handed me the axe she used for firewood and said, "Strike here."

So I swung at the wall and kept on hitting it until the axe struck something metal.

"Take out this box," she instructed.

My blows became a delicate excavation, which I widened in a circle until I found the edges of the box and was able to remove it. It was made of tin, and rusty. My mother explained softly, "The box was your grandmother's gift to us for our wedding, and what's inside was the gift from your grandfather and his brothers." Then she added, "Bring it to your grandfather."

It was heavy, and were it not for the darkness and the short distance, I would have opened it up on the way. But I was patient until I set it before Grandfather, who was surrounded by five of his sons and one of his sons-in-law. He opened it and took out a disassembled rifle and two pistols wrapped in rags that were wet from the petroleum grease smeared on the weapons.

Relatives were crowding into Grandfather's house, where tension showed on people's faces and strained their words. There was bitter coffee, war stories, and calls for manliness. They kept repeating the story of Grandfather with the dog when he was small, together with his maxim, as inspiration.

They made their plans in the light of incomplete information from some of those who had visited Tikrit recently, given that Grandfather didn't know anything about the city now. He said, "I used to know Tikrit when it was a small village, with its red earth covered with rats and its donkey-trading shepherds. So, where is the prison?"

They said, "We don't exactly know since there are so many buildings and police stations there now. Mustafa knows because they put him in prison two years ago for cursing the government in the sheep market."

"Bring me Mustafa," Grandfather replied.

We didn't sleep that night. The entire Mutlaq clan gathered together, along with all the villagers who had married into it. The house and the courtyard were packed with men getting their gear ready and loading their guns. Checkered kuffiyas were draped over their shoulders as their hands ran over their weapons, becoming reacquainted with how they worked. Meanwhile, the women busied themselves with cooking and bringing out equipment hidden in old cloth bags. And with whispering about what had happened to Istabraq. And with fear.

The children were playing a war game, and whenever they took a break to rest, their glances fell on the weapons between their fathers' hands, which they tried to touch by sitting quietly nearby until their fathers weren't paying attention or were preoccupied by conversation. Some of them pleaded with their mothers to tell their fathers to bring them along, but the mothers rebuffed them with decisive sharpness: "You're not going anywhere. This is serious business and not a game."

As the night drew on, the children slept in their mothers' arms, on their fathers' laps, or on the grass. The men sat in small groups while Grandfather reminded them of the raids of the first Muslims and recited the Qur'an until the first of the roosters announced the arrival of dawn. Grandfather rose and gave the order for the call to prayer. Then he led us in prayer as a group. I was seventeen years old at the time and considered one of the men.

We got in our cars and set off in a convoy to arrive at first light. We surrounded the provincial government building. My uncle fired a shot into the air, prompting the governor to come out onto the balcony behind the flower pots in his red-striped pajamas. He looked us over before disappearing to give orders to those inside to call the police and the central authorities. He came back into sight on the balcony, but this time he was wearing an elegant suit and necktie. Grandfather whispered into the ear of my uncle, who shouted out to the governor, "Give us Noah immediately! If you don't, we'll tear the building down around you!"

The governor called out nervously, "Please, come inside! Come now, friends, let's come to an understanding!"

Grandfather said to my uncle, "Tell him, 'There's nothing here for us to come to an understanding about. Give us our Noah and we'll return to our homes!'"

My uncle called out these sentences, circling his palms around his mouth like a funnel in order to amplify the sound.

The governor pushed his child, who had come out rubbing his eyes, back inside and called back, "Which Noah? I have no idea what you're talking about!"

Grandfather elbowed my uncle in the ribs, and they began climbing the main steps in front of the building until they disappeared into the darkness beyond the gates. The governor also disappeared from the balcony when he saw the two of them entering.

It was only ten minutes before the armored vehicles and police cars surrounded us, and two helicopters circled in the sky. A megaphone called to us from an unknown direction—maybe from all directions, from the sky, from the ground, and from behind the flower pots on the balcony: "Throw down your weapons and surrender!"

We were all wearing masks, and one of us responded with a shot, after which the air exploded in a roar of shots exchanged between the two sides. We learned afterward that the one who fired the first shot was my cousin Sirat, who was in love with my sister Istabraq. For that reason, he was the most zealous and angry of us all, and his aggression carried us all away. We all began firing at the armored vehicles in a tumult until we were shrouded by the smoke bombs that fell from the helicopters. Silence reigned, except for coughs and exchanged curses, which continued until we found ourselves in darkness: every one of us in a cell.

We received punches, kicks, lashes, and curses, and we could only respond with groans. The more they tortured me, the more I thought of Grandfather and feared for him. I kept asking them about him but was answered only with blows. They weren't even trying to interrogate me. I kept saying to myself, "He will certainly die if they are doing to him what they are doing to me." My body went numb from so much pain, and I was no longer strong enough to move. I lost consciousness many times under the blows, waking up to curses and cold water being splashed on me.

It went on until I thought I had been there being tortured for years—or was this the torment of the grave, which Grandfather had told us about? I kept wishing that it was all just a nightmare, that I would wake up afterward to my mother's breakfast of cream and butter on warm bread, dates fried in oil, and cardamom tea. Later we learned that the agony was for one day only, since that night they carried us out and threw us—bloody, groaning corpses piled on top of one another—into the beds of army trucks, after having shaved our hair and mustaches entirely off. The trucks set off amid a military convoy of nine armor-plated jeeps and continued until it reached the village in the middle of the night. There, our worried families were waiting on the rooftops of the houses.

The convoy stopped in the middle of the village, in the big square in front of the mosque. We used to play muhaybis and khawaytimi there at night when the month of Ramadan fell during the summer. It was also the place for village funerals, weddings, horse races, donkey races, and sack races—with the bags used for the cotton crop tied around our waists—as well as the high jump and the long jump. The police and the soldiers got down with their weapons and spread out across the square, while four of them began unloading us, carrying us out by our arms and legs. Before they threw us on the ground, they would bring each person to the captain. He would pull out of his pocket the new ID card that had been issued for each of us. They had changed all of our surnames from al-Mutlaq to al-Qashmar. In the Iraqi dialect, the word has the connotation of scorn, disdain, and insult, and it is applied to those who are said to be oblivious and stupid. In dictionaries of classical Arabic, which I paged through later, it means "short, stocky, piled up on itself."

I heard my name as I was being carried: "Saleem Noah al-Qashmar." Then I was thrown on the ground, and pain shot through my back.

When I regained consciousness, my mother said to me, "We thought you were dead, and that they were announcing the names of the bodies. We couldn't say a thing, we were so afraid."

"And Grandfather?" I asked.

She said, "He's fine. They didn't beat him too much. But they shaved his beard, his mustache, and his hair like everyone else."

We learned the following day that three of our men had been killed—Grandfather said "martyred"—in the clashes in the smoke in front of the provincial government building, while none of the police were injured. On the third day, we (the young men, at least) were able to get up and move around. I immediately visited Grandfather and had never seen him stronger or more angry. He was thinking of getting in touch with his friends among the elders of the other tribes and villages, men who had learned the Qur'an with him from Mullah Abd al-Hamid. He was also thinking about contacting his friends among the elders of the Kurdish tribes in Makhmur and Arbil, and the Turkish tribes in Kirkuk, and the Shabak people in al-Guwayr, and his Yazidi friends in Sinjar, who were tied to him by a long-lasting relationship of trust from his days as an onion merchant. Likewise, old friends among the Christians in Qarqush and Talkayf, who fought with him during the days of the British occupation. He thought of the chiefs of Najaf and Karbala, whom he had met when he used to travel there to acquire books, as well as his friends in Basra from his days of working in the docks there.

Grandfather was thinking of attacking again, and it seemed that the government had learned of these preparations, for they returned my father to Subh the next morning. His hair, beard, and mustache had been shaved, and his left leg was crippled: the foot was twisted and swollen with burns because they had applied electricity so many times. When he had begged them at least to transfer the wire to the right foot, they had put it on his testicles until they burned. The healing took a long time. When Noah did heal, he had become lame, and he never again fathered a child after the six of us. He gave up his dream of having twelve children.

Grandfather said to him, "He bit you."

My father replied, "I will bite him."

"How?" Grandfather asked.

My father took out of his pocket a bullet from the Tikrit boy's pistol, which he would later make into a keychain. He said, "I'll stick the remaining bullet in it." (He said "in it," and not "in his ass," because he would never, ever, dare breathe a coarse word in front of Grandfather.) "I will shave his head and his mustache, and I will tattoo or burn 'Qashmar' onto his forehead."

Grandfather said, "When?"

"I don't know. But I will most certainly do it."

Grandfather brought him a Qur'an and said, "Swear on this."

So my father put his hand on the book and took an oath, feeling satisfied in what he had resolved to do when he heard the satisfaction in Grandfather's voice. My father added, "The Bedouin man took his vengeance after forty years, and he said, 'I have made good time.'" My father was trying to show the seriousness of his resolve to fulfill his oath, however long it took.

Later on, we noticed the other families of the village, those who did not belong to our tribe, had begun to call us by our family nicknames, such as "Father of Saleem," or "Son of Noah," and not by our surnames, which was the usual way of things. Moreover, we realized that they did it only in front of us, out of respect for our feelings or else fearing a violent response. Their children, however, openly called our children "Qashmars" whenever there were quarrels, and they themselves, in our absence, used the official surname that the government had registered for us. So Grandfather, who hated hypocrisy, decided we would set off for a place all our own.

He spent a week thinking over the matter, gazing out the window of his sitting room at the Tigris River and Mount Makhul rising on the opposite bank, and repeating prayers for guidance before going to sleep. Then he said, "There."

During the night, we gathered all our belongings and put them in boats. When we reached the middle of the river, Grandfather called out to us, "Throw out every radio and television! Tear up all government documents and cast them in the river!"

We did so, feeling as though we were being liberated from some obscure burden that had been choking us. A woman trilled in joy when she saw how eagerly the men responded, and when she heard their remarks, such as the man who said, mockingly, "The river will carry our shredded papers down to them, and they can squeeze them out to make their tea!" He laughed, and everyone else did too.

We were fewer than one hundred people, together with several cats, dogs, chickens, and donkeys, and one horse. When we reached the shore and drew our boats up on the sand to secure them, we all stood under the moonlight and looked around. We were surrounded by the sound of waves, the rustling of trees, the howling of jackals, the croaking of frogs, and the chirping of grasshoppers in the nearby thickets.

Grandfather proclaimed, "O people of Mutlaq, be united as one! Show each other compassion, care for each other, and tend to your women and your flocks. Watch out for the hypocrites in the government: do not believe them, do not make friends with them, and do not allow any marriage ties with them. Build your world here according to what God wants and what you want. Do not ask the government for any documents or alms or property. As for the fuel and the medicine you need, barter for it with the people of Subh, but do not engage them in conversation, and do not ask them about anything at all.

"Never forget your vengeance!" (He looked at my father as he said this.) "When the number of your men exceeds seventy—the number of the Prophet's companions in the Battle of Badr and the number of his grandson Hussein's companions at Karbala—start blowing up the pillars of government! Strike them with an iron fist, wherever you are able! Bear patiently the disgrace of your surname Qashmar until you take revenge. For I fear you would forget your rightful claim if you forgot the insulting name.

"Let the Qur'an be your school; let hunting and swimming be your sport; let the truth guide your words; let freedom be your goal; let patience be your mode of life; let honesty be your language; let work be your habit; and let remembrance be your rule! Do not lie down to sleep before you absolutely need to. I declare it unlawful for you to eat food made in factories, to work for the tyrannical government, to wear the uniform of the police, or to spill each other's blood.

"Now come! Let us build a village that we will call Qashmars today so that we will not forget. And after the vengeance, we will call it Freedmen, or Dignity, or The Absolute. O God, maintain our love for freedom and for human dignity. Kill us as you want or as we want, not as our enemies want! Amen, O Lord of the worlds!"

We all responded, according to the ritual, and with all our hearts, "Amen!"

In the silence of the night, the echo reverberated off the mountain, the forest, and the bend in the river. An "Amen!" swelling like the voice of millions of pilgrims or an army preparing for war. Our fervor and the majesty of the echo intensified Grandfather's zeal. He continued the prayer, leaving us a space of silence after each phrase for us to give it our "Amen!"

"O God, we seek your protection from weakness and sloth. (Amen!)

"We seek your protection from cowardice and greed. (Amen!)

"We seek your protection from debt and from men triumphing over us. (Amen!)

"We seek your protection from need, except for you, from lowliness, except before you, and from fear, except of you. (Amen!)

"We seek your protection from the worst of mankind, from worry for our daily bread, and from wicked ways. (Amen!)

"We seek your protection from our enemies taking joy in our pain, from the illness that doesn't go away, and from the crushing of our hopes, O most merciful of all merciful ones, O Lord of the worlds! (Amen! A-a-men!)"

Then we carried our things and pressed into the forest, everyone seeking a spot upon which to build his new home. And to this day, I still hear the echo of that "Amen," awesome like nothing else.

CHAPTER 2

I loved my father without understanding him. I sensed there was more than one Noah inside of him, but he was able to harmonize them perfectly.

My mother's duality, however, was clear. This made it all the easier to love her, even though I only realized the magnitude of my love for her when I was away from her, during my time in the army and now too in my exile. She was always there to absorb our anger, and to share in our pain and our joy. She always took care of preparing our food, washing our clothes, and reminding us of our responsibilities. She passed on the orders of the older children to the younger and prevented the older ones from hitting them. She lulled us to sleep with the narrative rhythms of princesses falling in love, female ghouls, monsters, giants, and Sinbad.

Meanwhile, it was beyond me to understand my cousin Aliya even for a day. I loved her unconditionally, without any real reason, only that she had loved me without any hard questions. It was from her that I learned how to love—quite the opposite of everyone else, who considered Grandfather Mutlaq to be

15

the only possible teacher. But I now realize that the lessons we learned from him didn't shape our essential selves nearly as much as having adopted him as our inexorable standard did. He was an adversary who forced us to sculpt our private selves in secret.

My father was the eldest of his siblings, so the greatest burden fell on him. Not only the burden of work but also of Grandfather's notions about a strict upbringing, that a child should be nourished on the concept of blind obedience to parents: "God's satisfaction comes from the satisfaction of parents."

Noah never once refused a request or a command from his father. I remember, for example, how he returned at noon one day in July, exhausted from his work at the oil company in Kirkuk. He would usually go to the guest room first to greet Grandfather (who had lived there alone with his books ever since Grandmother died) and then come to the house to kiss us and shake hands with Mother. On that day, Grandfather ordered him to go repair the broken water pump at the farm. So he left his bag and headed out to the field immediately, without stopping at the house on his way to greet us, bathe, rest, and eat his lunch as he usually did. He didn't return until he had repaired the pump, just as the sun was setting.

My father never met Grandfather's eyes and never even looked at his face. He would always stare at the ground, listening intently to Grandfather's words. He was more than forty years old, yet he said he was ashamed to look into his father's face. One quiet day, near the banks of the river, he asked me, curious and almost entreating, "How do you look at his face? Have you looked into his eyes? Have you looked into his eyes?"

I wish that I could ask him now, "Then how could you kill him? And how did you arrive here? When? Why exactly did you come to Spain? Was it that you came looking for me?" But his first embrace had been neutral, not to say cold. As if he hadn't even wanted to hug me.

I found my father by chance last Saturday night in Madrid. On weekends, I feel a discontent steal into my soul, and I wander through the dark streets and alleys without any fixed destination. I'll go into any club or bar. This time, I absolutely couldn't believe what I saw in a club packed with people of various nationalities—immigrants, tourists, and of course Spaniards—as well as hippies, homosexuals, outcasts, hashish dealers, night owls, pacifists, racists, anti-globalization activists, and skinheads.

This man with the shaved mustache. A receding hairline. Long hair tied in a ponytail, with two small locks dyed red and green. Three silver loops hung down from his left ear— earrings. Could he possibly be my father?! Was this really my father?! Then he showed me his keychain, which we had gotten used to seeing after our attack on the provincial government building in Tikrit. The keychain was a small revolver bullet. He had emptied out the gunpowder and inserted a ring through the case, to which he attached a chain for his keys. I kept staring doubtfully into his face, so he quickly showed me his lame foot, after which I was certain. We embraced.

When? How? Why did my father come to Madrid? This chance meeting dazed me for three days. After that, I started to regain my equilibrium as I digested the surprise, content to ignore the incomprehensible. Like how I keep returning to paintings by Salvador Dalí in order to understand reality better.

After my flight from the confines of Iraq ten years ago, I had reconciled myself to forgetting in order to reconcile myself to life. I didn't realize I was putting into effect my village's ultimate decision to detach itself completely. No letters between me and it. No news reaching me, and none of me reaching it. My father was the last person I saw there. Unnoticed, I saw him through the window of the mosque before I left at dawn without a farewell. After that, I saw no one else from my village, and I convinced myself with absolute certainty that I would never see any of them. The village would never see me, and I would never again see it. Even had I wanted to, it would never welcome me back, for I had betrayed it when I abandoned it in secret after the seventeen bodies began to rot and the air became intolerable.

That was the reason that I began avoiding foul odors, because they would remind me of all the details I was sometimes happy to forget entirely. I would take out the trash before the garbage bags filled up. I chose fifth-floor apartments in order to live far from the putrid sewer lines in the ground. I sprayed air freshener in the bathroom and deodorant in my armpits. I avoided going past police stations and government buildings, and I didn't follow the news in the media.

But my father brought it all back with his sudden presence here and his constant repetition of a phrase unlike anything I could have imagined him saying, him being so proper, timid, and religious: "This world is all fucked up." And when I gave in to this presence of his and asked him about our village, Qashmars, he said, "The whole world is Qashmars."

The village of Qashmars began with my father, and at his hands it would later be saved from entering the dungeons of the security forces a second time. With the death—or the murder—of Grandfather, he had put it to an end. Now once again, it began at his hands, here in a dim Madrid club. On its door was written "Club Qashmars." Below that in a smaller script, "In the beginning was freedom: May it endure till the end!" Below that, in the same size lettering but in blue, "The freer you feel, the greater your welcome here."

I wanted to ask my father about many things: Mother, my siblings, my childhood friends, our village after the seventeen corpses, and about my cousin Aliya—no, Aliya drowned in the river. (Why do I not want to believe that despite seeing it with my own eyes?) I wanted to ask him whether he really killed Grandfather.

But he still didn't say much, and every time I went to see him at the club in the evening, I found him surrounded by a group of his friends—Spaniards, Dutch, Germans, and English. Most of them had hair that was shaved or combed—messed up, that is—in unusual styles, which they stained with brilliant dyes. Bunches of keys hung from their belts, along with chains like those used to tie up pet dogs. Bits of metal were set into every part of their strange clothing, and loops of silver or plastic hung from their ears and even the noses and navels of some of them.

My father fit right in. He wore a mesh shirt with vivid camouflage, and he had attached three rings to his left ear, each larger than the previous one. But instead of cutting his hair like the others to resemble a rooster, a lion, or a sheep, he had let grow it long. Mild balding had set in at his forehead, and he tied his hair back in a ponytail, like a schoolgirl, dyeing two locks, one of them green and the other red.

Was this really my father? The people circling around him, boisterous with laughter, with smoke, and slapping each other's thighs, were all young, with the exception of a woman in her forties. He embraced her from time to time, and she would kiss him. This woman was very talkative, just the opposite of him, and her laughter rose above everyone else's. She told me her name was Rosa, and that she was from Barcelona, but she was here in Madrid because she loved my father.

Three days passed, and I wasn't able to get him alone. I would invite him to a café or to come over to my place: "I live here, close by, on Fomento Street, about ten minutes away."

To which he would reply, "Tomorrow."

When I would ask the next day, he would say, "Tomorrow," and he would apologize for the day before. "I'm very busy, Saleem, as you can see. But I promise you, tomorrow. Tomorrow, for sure."

He didn't call me "son," and he didn't say "God willing," as would be normal for an Arab.

This kept on until I came one day, and before I could even open my mouth, he said, "Come on, I'll give you a haircut."

Without waiting for my response, he pulled a small stool from one of the corners into the middle of the dance floor, amid the debris of the previous night. I sat down. He called out, "Fatumi, bring me my clippers!"

The dark-skinned girl behind the bar stopped washing the glasses and took down a box from one of the shelves behind her. She brought it over to him, saying, "Here you are, sir."

"Thanks," he said, and before she moved away he gave her a gentle pat on the butt.

She returned to the glasses, and I asked, "Is she Arab?"

He said, "Fatima? Yes, Moroccan. A good girl."

The rest of the staff, two Spanish girls, were going back and forth around us, reminding Rosa about the drinks, napkins, and cigarette packs that had run out. Noah was giving them directions with gestures and smiles, with the clippers in his hand over my head. His Barcelona girlfriend kept coming in and out, carrying account books. She was calling distribution companies for beer and other drinks, then asked the fruit and nut shop to send her twenty kilograms of olives, another twenty of dried fruit, and ten of sunflower seeds ("And quickly!"). She also called a cigarette distributor to supply her with a carton of each kind, a box of lighters, and a box of gum ("And quickly!"). They did indeed come quickly, and Rosa directed the workers to quit cleaning ("Right away!") and to stock the deliveries instead. My father stopped cutting my hair to oversee their work.

When he saw that things were proceeding as he wanted, he asked me, "And how are you doing? What do you do for work?"

"I'm fine," I said. "I work as a driver for a newspaper distribution company. From six till eleven in the morning."

He asked, "Do you have a woman?"

"No," I replied.

He called something over to Rosa in a mixture of English and Arabic, and I caught the Arabic word for "tip," baksheesh. I turned around to see her resisting with a scowl on her face and a wink, so he drew out her name to insist, "Ro-o-osa. . . ."

She gave in and went to the cash register. We all heard the clink of the coins that she put in the palm of the man who had brought in the cases of beer. Then my father resumed cutting my hair and asked me, "What do you do with your free time?"

I said, "I read. Sometimes I write. I go to the movies."

He asked, "Have you read Lorca and Alberti in Spanish?"

"Yes," I said, "but I don't like their poetry very much. I like Juan Ramón Jiménez and Vicente Aleixandre better."

"Unfortunately, I still don't speak Spanish," he said. "Only a few words. What do you write, poetry?"

"A few poems. But I'm better at short stories. I've published a few of them in the Iraqi opposition newspapers in London."

He was curious and surprised: "The opposition?"

I thought I would make use of writing as a way to ask about Grandfather's books, about our village, Mother, my siblings, my childhood friends, my cousin—no, my cousin Aliya is dead—and about Grandfather's murder. So I said, "I'm thinking about writing a novel about our village, but I'm reluctant to expose its shame."

He said, "Write whatever you want. Nothing will happen worse than has already happened. This world is all fucked up."

It was the first time I had heard my father use a word like this. I realized then that many changes had come over his personality. There was a lot he was hiding, important experiences that he had undergone in the past ten years when I had been away from him. I wanted to ask him about how he had arrived here and about this Rosa. But he gave my head a playful smack and said, "There! All done. Take yourself off to the bathroom to wash your head."

When I passed in front of the bar, Fatima smiled. Her two lips were like a split fig, as Herman Hesse says in *Siddhartha*. She had wide, black eyes, and the thickness of her lashes made them all the more enchanting as she wiped a glass with her apron. I smiled at her too, without forgetting my father's hand on her butt just minutes before. In the bathroom, I was surprised by my reflection in the mirror with a shaved head. Had he used the number one attachment, maybe even zero? I looked like some of his friends and nighttime customers.

I rubbed my head like someone feeling a strange egg. I had never cut my hair like this except when I was in the army and had no choice in the matter. Sergeant Khazaal had seemed intoxicated by cutting our hair the moment we entered camp. In the hands of the barbers, our heads were an amusing toy that they turned violently in all directions, roughly and happily, as though intending to provoke us.

22

For a minute, I felt how strange I looked, but I resolved not to think about it for long. The thing that interested me was getting close to my father and having an open conversation with him. I put my head under the tap in the sink and scrubbed as the cold water poured down. I came back up looking for a piece of soap, but I didn't find one. I brought my head back down under the stream of water telling myself that this was good enough to remove the rest of the hair clippings, and that I would take a shower when I got back to my apartment.

When I brought my head up again, I found Fatima standing beside me, smiling in the mirror. She had a towel in her hand, which she held out to me, saying, "Nice haircut!"

Her full lips in the middle of her light brown skin were like African drawings, and her wide eyes were accentuated by eyeliner and the black of her lashes.

"Thanks," I said. I tried to look at her breasts since that was what most attracted me in women ever since the first time I fell in love, with my cousin Aliya, who used to smear dates on her breasts for me to suck off. But Fatima turned, going back to wash the glasses, and I saw her butt, together with the image of my father's hand spanking it gently.

I dried my head and looked in the mirror. "Not too bad," I said to myself, and I went out.

My father was in the corner of the stage organizing the microphone cords. He said, "Do you want me to dye it blond for you?"

I heard him perfectly well, but I still asked, "What?"

He repeated, "I could dye it for you—yellow, for instance."

"No," I said, "This is enough. It's great like this." Then I added, "I'm going to take off. Do you want to come with me?"

He took the broom from the corner and said, "No, I'm busy now. Leave it for another time. Tomorrow, for example."

"Fine," I said. "I'm going then. Thanks for the haircut." I went over to the bar and gave Fatima the towel, looking at her eyes, at her . . . . I still wasn't able to see her breasts because she was wiping a glass with her apron.

"Thanks," she said with a smile. I couldn't separate from her the image of my father spanking her butt. I would see her; then I would see it.

At the stairs going up to the exit, Rosa was still giving the girls instructions about places to clean or where to put the deliveries. I said goodbye to them, and before I got too far from the door, Rosa called out to me, "Come back in the evening! It's going to be a beautiful party!"

"I don't know," I said. "We'll see. See you later."

I walked through the alleys leading to Plaza de Santo Domingo, planning to cross it on my way home. Meanwhile, my father had taken hold of my brain with his "this world is all fucked up" and his hand spanking Fatima's butt. How could he do that, he being the one that dragged us into battle against the government merely because one of them had touched the butt of my sister Istabraq? I kept trying to pull together what I remembered of him in order to understand these changes. Certainly he was my father: the voice, the tall body with solid muscles, the lame foot, the bullet keychain, and . . . .

I had to put my thoughts in order, so I wandered over to a coffee shop at the end of the square. Sitting in front of the bartender and leaning on the bar, I ordered café con leche and a glass of water. I took out a cigarette and smoked it, inhaling with long, slow drags. In the mirror across from me, I saw my face framed between two bottles. I rubbed my head, but I didn't focus on my new haircut too much since the thing that occupied my attention was my father.

My new father. I tried to find an explanation for what had happened, to prepare myself to accept the breadth of his new reality. He was my father, no question. I remembered my entire relationship with him well. I knew his former personality, which I had left in our village in Iraq ten years ago. He was my father, even though he now seemed to be a completely different person. Take it easy, Saleem! Yes, just take it easy. I tried to put the picture in order.

CHAPTER 3

Like the rest of my siblings, I never called him "Father" until I was ten, when I was able to make the distinction. Before then, we would call him by his first name, "Noah," and we would call Grandfather "Father." That was because Grandfather was the one who was always home with us.

My father, on the other hand, was usually away, working in the oil companies in Kirkuk. He only came to us on weekends, carrying his bag filled with gifts, foreign books, and dirty clothes. Whenever Mother wanted to encourage us to work harder, she would say, "Look at your father. He was a young man of your age when he began working in Kirkuk. I remember that day, exactly one month and two days after our wedding. More than twenty years ago."

He had begun as a night watchman, then became a metal worker, and then a mechanic. He did so well in his language classes that they appointed him as a supervisor for the workers, and as a translator and intermediary between the German managers and the Iraqi laborers.

It was never important for Noah to make us understand his relationship to us. He had entrusted our upbringing to Grandfather, just as he kept obeying and entrusting his own personality to him until Grandfather's death (or until he killed him!). Likewise, he didn't introduce me as his son here in his club. He said "Saleem" instead. Just "Saleem." He might have filled in Rosa about that afterward, seeing as she started treating me with a special, sometimes even excessive, affection.

My father—or Noah—was massively built. He had powerful muscles but a calm demeanor. Grandfather, on the other hand, was a skinny old man who supported himself with a magnificent bamboo cane, the top of which was the carved head of an eagle with blue beads for eyes. It had been given to him by a Pakistani friend, whom he had met on a pilgrimage to Mecca as they circled around the Ka'aba. But Grandfather only used this cane of his after scratching away the features of the eagle's head, turning it into simply a ball or an egg. Since he wasn't able to pull out the two beads of its eyes, he had been content to deface them with the tip of the knife from a pair of fingernail clippers.

"No!" we protested. "Why, Grandfather?"

He said, "These are idols, and whoever fashions the image of a living creature will be asked by God in the hereafter to animate it with life. And given that he will be unable to do so— because that is one of the special powers of God alone—he will then receive his punishment."

Mother said that Grandfather had been massive and powerful like my father. In this way she reassured herself that my father's potbelly would shrink and he would become slender again over time. She didn't realize that Grandfather was so thin because he had come down with diabetes on account of his craze for devouring sweets and dates. Our house was never without a bag of dates propped up in one of the corners and a box of bride's fingers desserts tucked between his books.

The death of my grandmother, his third wife, had also had an effect on him. He had begun to wither and dry up, little by little, like the udder of a sick cow, until he became very skinny. But the power of his spirit and his voice had not been affected. Perhaps, if anything, they had increased and compensated for the loss of his bodily strength. That strength was transformed into the commands he imposed on others with such stern conviction that they would carry out whatever he wanted.

His cane, when he swung it, was no less dreadful than himself. We would hear the air whistle around it, threatening violence every time he grew angry or gave an order. We used to fear both him and it, even though we never saw him hit anyone. It might be that our imaginations magnified his dreadfulness beyond what it would have been had we actually experienced his blows.

What increased our conception of his violent anger, besides the recollection of him biting the dog's neck when he was small, was the story of him cutting off the finger of his first wife when they quarreled one month after their marriage. She had raised her voice against him and warned that she would complain to her brother Hamad, pointing her finger at him in a threatening gesture. Swelling up in pride, Mutlaq flew into a burning rage. He grabbed her index finger just above the first knuckle and picked up a knife that was beside him on the edge of the stove. He chopped the finger off at the knuckle and shoved the severed fingertip into her pocket. It was the size of a small stone or a date, its blood draining out.

Grandfather set her on her donkey, which she had brought as a gift from her family on the occasion of their wedding, and drove her out of the village. All the while, she held her amputated finger, shrieking and looking at both it and Grandfather, unable to believe what she saw. He pointed her in the direction of her village and said, "Give your finger to your brother Hamad. Tell him, 'This is my finger, which I used to threaten Mullah Mutlaq in your name.' You are hereby divorced irrevocably!"

He struck her donkey sharply on the withers, and it set off at a trot, leaving behind drops of her blood in its hoof prints. She never returned, and it is said that Hamad told her, "You deserved it. How could you ever threaten your husband? If I were in his place, I would have done the same!"

As for his second wife, we didn't know anything about her except that she died of cancer without bearing any children. The third wife, my grandmother, was the one that had provided him with all nine of his children, the eldest of whom was Noah.

Grandfather took upon himself the naming of his children, his grandchildren, and all those connected to his lineage, but he said, "It is God who chose your names, not I." That was because as soon as one of us was born, he would perform the ritual ablutions and pray two prostrations. Then he would sit at the head of the newborn and open the Qur'an at random. Looking at the face of the child, or else closing his eyes, he would put his finger on the page, and whatever word his finger landed on would be the name. If it happened to be a preposition or if there wasn't anything in the verse that suited the baby's gender, he would close his eyes again and move his finger to another place on the same page.

So it was, to give an example, that the Qur'an opened to the first page of the sura entitled *The Night Journey* when my father was born. The finger fell and indicated the verse: *The descendants of those whom we carried with Noah; verily, he was a grateful servant.* When my mother bore twin girls, Sundus and Istabraq, his finger fell on verse 31 of *The Cave*: *Those people have the gardens of Eden, under which the rivers flow. Golden bracelets are bound upon them, and they wear green garments of refined silk (sundus) and brocade (istabraq), reclining there on couches. How excellent is their reward, and how lovely the resting place!* My cousin Aliya's name came from *The Ultimate Reality,* in verses 22-23: *In a lofty (aliya) garden whose grapes hang low.* As for me, the Qur'an opened to *The Poets,* and his finger fell on the following verse: *A day when neither wealth nor sons will be of any use, except for those who come to God with a sound (saleem) heart.*

I don't know whether "The Poets" had a role in my relationship to poetry. I would read poetry frequently and desperately try to write it, despite my fading hope that I would become a well-known and important poet, as I used to dream when I was young. Or perhaps Aliya was my most important influence, in that I wrote it for her sake? I sent her my first poems with Istabraq, and she became frightened of me.

Grandfather was part of the reason too, for he used to tell us stories of knights who were lovers and poets, and he would recite some of their poems, which were filled with horses, the night, the desert, swords, and the flying heads of enemies. And maybe I was also attracted to poetry because of my father, who had memorized Goethe's *Poems of the East and the West* in German, even if he didn't understand all the words. His German friend Kristof, head of the division of workers in one of the Kirkuk oil companies, had given it to him, saying, "Read this. He was one of us, but he loved your prophet." So my father memorized it one weekend, going back and forth on the banks of the Tigris River, waving his arms, imagining an audience in the waves, the pebbles, and the willow trees.

At that time I was a little boy, spying on him from the cliff over the river. I imagined that he was preparing for an exam since my eldest brother, Hakeem, would do the same thing during the days of his exams. One of the times that my father turned to face his audience, he caught sight of me and called me over. I hurried down to him. He sat on a rock and hung his feet in the water, setting me on his knees. He spoke admiringly about Goethe and translated some passages from his book for me. I didn't understand anything because I was focused on my wish to be big like him so that my feet would reach the water. Just like how I would put off trying to understand things in general until I was older.

My father was repeating, "The Germans are an amazing people. Imagine: Kristof is my boss at work, but he is also my friend! He says to me, 'Your people invented the phoenix with your imagination, and mine personified it in the world.' His wife, Sabina, is blond and beautiful. She writes poetry and joins us in the oil work. The Germans are an amazing people, Saleem, an amazing people."

Because of how frequently my father spoke to me about the Germans, I used to imagine that they were like the people of Paradise, whom Grandfather would describe for us: "In Paradise, which we will enter in the afterlife, everyone is young. Everyone is one hundred feet tall. No one becomes sick, grows old, or dies. They eat what they want, when they want it. They point a finger at any bird, and it falls from the branches of the trees of Paradise; it is placed on a plate in front of them to eat, grilled and delicious; they eat as much as they want; then the bird's bones reassemble, and in an instant it regains its form and lives again, returning to its branch. We will not defecate there. On the contrary, we will sweat perfume. We will have

31

magnificent forms, and we will have beautiful women from among the nymphs of Paradise: if one of them peeked out from the sky right now, the light of her face would illuminate the earth. We will lie with them, but they will regain their virginity. To drink, we will dip our hand into rivers of wine, honey, milk, and whatever the soul desires."

I imagined them in this way because my father never tired of saying, "The Germans are an amazing people." He learned German and English from the foreigners at the oil companies. He memorized passages of Shakespeare's *Hamlet* as well. Of course, he had also memorized the entire Qur'an because Grandfather was intent on making all of us memorize it. He said that it would be our closest friend in the desolation of the grave, and an advocate to defend us before the court of the two angels, Munkar and Nakeer: "When a person dies, he is buried and abandoned all alone. Then the two angels come and examine him. Therefore, if they ask you who is your lord, say, 'God'; about your prophet, say, 'Muhammad'; about your religion, say, 'Islam'; and about your book, say, 'The Qur'an.'"

Among all the members of our family, my father was the only one who kept the complete Qur'an preserved in his memory. Therefore, Grandfather would ask his help as he advanced in years and his memory began to fail him. As for us, the children of the next generation, we memorized some sections and forgot them, with the exception of the shorter suras and the verses associated with our names because Grandfather was intent on each of us knowing at least the verse from which our name had sprung.

He would say, "God was the one who chose your names, and their source is here in his book. Look!" Then he would point out for each of us the verse with his finger, as though he were reenacting for us the scene of our own naming, which we had not seen.

Many of the people of our village followed this naming method of his. For some of them, fate brought a rare and beautiful name, while for others, the name entailed problems and psychological suffering. An example of that was Aunt Huda's son, whose father's finger fell upon the word sirat ("path"). When we were small and quarreled with Sirat as we played, we would call him dirat ("fart"). In school, whenever he left the room and we could get hold of his notebooks, we would change his name by adding a dot over the letter saad to make it a daad. As a result, he grew up to be the opposite of his peaceful nature and his family's reserved disposition. He became a fierce boy who would get into many fights, tortured by bearing this name that didn't give him any rest until his corpse came back with those of my brother Hakeem and three of my cousins among the seventeen decomposing bodies.

We used to pick on Sirat and provoke him, then run away. When he realized that we had escaped his grasp, or when the stones he threw didn't reach us, he would yell in a loud, agonized voice, "Are you making fun of the name that God gave me? Don't you fear going to hell? Are you laughing at the painter or the painting?"

That would make us truly ashamed, and we did become afraid of God and pray for forgiveness because we were reminded of a story Grandfather had told us about a man whose name was Malik bin Dinar ("King, son of Gold Coin"). At the time, we had laughed at the name Dinar, only to be scolded by Grandfather before he continued his story. Malik was going along the road one day when he happened upon a donkey (or a dog—I don't remember exactly now). The donkey was colored in a strange way: white with black spots on its eyes, ears, stomach, and tail. Malik burst out laughing, but then the donkey turned to him and spoke in a human voice, saying, "Are you laughing at the painter or the painting?" Malik immediately understood the reference to the Creator and the donkey. He fell to his knees and prostrated himself in repentance. He kept crying for forty years and asking God's forgiveness for the mockery and scorn that he had shown one of his creatures. In the end, after he spent forty years weeping and showing special attention to every donkey he saw, God forgave him.

Only that sentence—"Are you laughing at the painter or the painting?"—could keep us from harassing Sirat. But we would quickly forget it and just as quickly resume our bullying. It continued like that until he died and received his rest—from us and from his name.

Sirat loved my sister Istabraq, and for that reason he was the most zealous of us all on the day of the attack against the provincial government building in Tikrit, when three of us were killed (Grandfather said "martyred"). Afterward, Istabraq became even more emaciated. Feeling guilty for their deaths, she refused to eat, and whenever Mother forced her to drink chicken soup, she would vomit it up. She became skinnier and skinnier, to the point where we could see her continually wasting away. She was receding from us little by little in the bed, sinking into it like someone disappearing into the horizon. The bulges of her shoulder blades jutted out, along with the joints of her fingers and the bony balls in her wrists. Sirat's sisters stopped calling her "Reed," and stopped addressing Sirat as "Reed-lover," for "it's just not right to have fun at the expense of the sick." And what's more, she had become much skinnier than she was when they gave her this nickname.

Grandfather said, "In that case, forget the doctors. The only hope is in the remedy of God, the Healer and Caretaker, and of his righteous saints. One of my close friends is a Kurd-ish sheikh who lives in a village near Shaqlawa and possesses miraculous powers. He is in the Naqshbandiya Sufi tradition, and his ancestors trace their descent back to Sheikh Abd al-Qadir al-Kilani, who struck an infidel in India with his sandal without moving from where he sat in Baghdad."

So we took her there, my father, Grandfather, and I. I was sitting with Istabraq in the back seat of the car, supporting her on my shoulder and giving her water to drink. At the same time, I was enjoying the view of green fields flying past on both sides. After my father stopped a few times to ask about the road, the village, and the sheikh's house, the man's fame became obvious to us because everyone knew immediately how to direct us. We drove the car up to his house, which sat at the foot of a mountain on the outskirts of the village.

As soon as we got out in the front courtyard, we heard the clap of a gunshot coming from the direction of his door. Ista-braq immediately fell out of my arms and lay stretched out on the ground, unconscious.

Then we heard Grandfather's roar, "God is great!"

CHAPTER 4

I didn't leave my apartment the whole evening. I ate three eggs and some salad since I didn't feel like cooking. I spent time thinking about my father and remembering, trying to work out what had happened so that I might understand my new father who was here. I got up more than once from my bed, heading to the kitchen to make coffee and smoke cigarettes in the window that overlooked the square courtyard, small and deep, enclosed by my building. Lines stretched between the windows for hanging out the wash to dry. In the courtyard below, there was a small, wooden doghouse for the dog belonging to one of the old women on the first floor.

I'm the youngest resident of the building. Next is a young Cuban woman with dark skin who lives below me; my floor is her ceiling. Meanwhile, old women occupy the other apartments. They are on their own, and the only company they have is their dogs, to whom they speak day and night, and the television hosts reporting on celebrity scandals. After the stance I took regarding the trash, these women started looking at me suspiciously whenever we would meet on the stairs. Their misgivings increased when I refused to meet with the neighbors' council to discuss repairing the lock of the main door. I said to the doorman: "There's no need for this waste of time. You go, yourself, and buy a new lock to install. Then collect its cost from the building's residents."

That was because I thought their free time made these meetings an occasion to gossip, complain, and satisfy their curiosity by scrutinizing the rest of the neighbors from up close. I had decided not to attend these neighbors' meetings ever since the first year.

We had met one evening, crowded into the foyer. Some of us sat on the first flight of stairs, while the doorman kept clicking the lights back on after they would automatically go out every minute. The meeting revolved around the garbage can and the fact that some people didn't pay the monthly fee for the doorman to take it out each night and bring it back in the morning.

Their eyes sought me out, along with gossip veiled in courtesy. Despite my calm nature, and my desire to avoid confrontations with anyone, I don't put up with other people trying to take advantage of me. So everyone was surprised when I announced quite openly that, while it was necessary for those people who owned their apartments to pay their share, I wouldn't pay for the trash can since the landlord paid for renters, just as was spelled out in the rental contract. The old women burst out talking among themselves and raising objections, especially those who owned their apartments. At the same time, the other renters thanked me for pointing this out, including the Cuban girl, who became my friend after that.

She and I would stop for a while every time we met on the stairs. We commiserated about the ruling dictatorships in our countries. She vented to me about her sufferings here on account of not having legal residency papers. This meant she worked without contracts and moved frequently between one job and another, where she would be exploited by her bosses. I invited her more than once to drink tea in my apartment, and she invited me to her birthday party. Every time she received one of her acquaintances escaping from "The Island of Sugar," she would bring me coarse Havana cigarettes as a gift. We exchanged music recordings. We would also turn to each other if we needed salt, sugar, oil, or an onion.

The Cuban stopped paying for the trash, and, like me, she became an object of suspicious glances from the old women. Several times I heard them curse the current government for having opened the gates of the country to foreigners, and they nostalgically praised the days of Franco. More than once, I even heard one of them singing the old version of the national anthem with Franco's lyrics, "Viva España," for an entire morning, intentionally leaving her window open so that the neighbors would hear. Even worse, she would sometimes deliberately stretch her arm out the window in the manner of the Nazi salute.

The doorman, however, kept treating me affectionately because I would always give him gifts at Christmas: gloves, a shirt, a jacket, cigarettes, newspapers. I remember one Friday after coming back from the mosque I also gave him a box of Middle Eastern sweets as a gift. He was very happy with it.

Two days after the meeting about the trash can, one of the women stopped me on the stairs and said in a threatening tone, "This won't do. You have to pay. We are in Spain, not in your country. There are laws here."

What could I say to this? Would she even understand if I told her that the first law in the world had been decreed by an Iraqi, Hammurabi, in his stele? Her tone, her words, the twitching of her jaw, and the hairs coming out of her nose all provoked me.

"Fine," I replied. "If you have a right over me in anything, make a formal complaint, and obtain your rights according to this law that you are talking about."

She was silent for a little while. Then she burst into imploring tears. "I'm a widow who's all alone, and my pension is small. My dog died two months ago, and no one came to comfort me. I'm heartbroken over him, and I cry more than I cried for my husband. Sonny—my dog—was a good dog. Whenever I came in, he would wag his tail and welcome me joyfully. He would go with me for my daily walk around the park. He was—"

I interrupted her when I realized that she was prepared to spend the entire day talking about the virtues of her dead dog. "I'm sorry, ma'am. I'm in a hurry and am waiting for a phone call."

The flow of her tears stopped, and she said in a different tone altogether, "So will you contribute to the payment?"

"No," I said. "Excuse me, goodbye."

Then I turned and went up the stairs without looking back. Behind me, I heard her muttering words that were certainly insults because she slammed her door afterward. What could I say to this old woman, who was older than my mother by perhaps twenty years, and nevertheless looked healthier than her and hadn't stopped putting on makeup? How could I make her understand the deaths of my brothers, my cousins, Grandfather, and my beloved Aliya, not to mention the castration of my father and the wars, while she was shedding tears over a dog?

After that, all of them started keeping their distance with the exception of my friend, the Cuban. But I kept taking the initiative to greet them whenever I ran into them on the stairs, in the lobby, or at the bread and fruit shop across from our building. Some of them didn't return the greeting at first, but as time went on, they became content to exchange pleasantries and leave me alone, not inviting me to any further meetings.

I was more comfortable with this isolation: it's what I wanted. I would enter my apartment, my world, where I lived among my books, my kitchen, my music, and my efforts to improve my Spanish. I would cut out any picture about Iraq that I found in the newspapers. For a period of ten years I hung these up in the apartment, until in the end they crowded the walls of my bedroom, the living room, the hallway, and the kitchen. It was unfortunate that the newspapers would only publish tragic photos of Iraq, such as destroyed buildings, burned-out tanks, flies in the busy markets, and pictures of the dictator's image in the streets and courtyards and on building façades. For that reason, I did my best to select the least grim of them. I hung them everywhere except the spot where I prayed, behind the living room door. They were all black and white apart from two color postcards, one from Tunis with palm trees, and the other sent to me by my friend from Iran, with minarets and golden domes in the style of the holy city of Karbala. I also had the colorful cover of a Spanish newspaper, which had been designed by computer: a map of Iraq that had fighter jets pointing their tips at it.

I was content in this world of mine where I lived out my first identity, my nostalgia, and my longing for my mother's embraces, for my siblings, for a visit to Aliya's grave, for swimming in the Tigris River, for my friends, for our cows, donkeys, chickens, and for the mountain. I yearned for news from them, news about them. How were they now? What had happened? What was happening? Who among them had died? Who had married whom, and what children had they had? What were the new names there? Was it still God—or their finger on the Qur'an—that chose for everyone his name and special verse? I would listen only to Arabic music, and I cooked Iraqi meals.

I had endured much in order to arrive here, and I endured more in order to establish legal residency and to find a way to support myself. I liked living here amid this freedom and this peace. Therefore, when I was out of my apartment, I was one of them, from this place, and I took an interest in what they were interested in: soccer matches, bull fights, celebrity gossip, staying up late on weekends. But when I returned to my apartment, alone, I was from my people, from there.

So it was until my father suddenly appeared, different from the one I left there, different from the one who lived with me in my memories throughout these years. For where would I situate him according to my bifurcated world? His former image was firmly established within my inner world: my memory, the apartment, these black-and-white pictures, and blood relations. But now I see that he does not belong to it. At the same time, I can't exactly consider him part of my outside world.

His friends here were not like my friends. His work was not like mine, nor his behavior. Indeed, he did not resemble himself. His women did not resemble my women. Or at least, they did not resemble those I had met, since I didn't have women for the most part—or at all. The only woman I had gone out with during my time here was Pilar.

I met Pilar six years ago, when I went one weekend to a club with my friends, who were my co-workers. She was introduced to me by Antonio, who was responsible for reviewing

41

the addresses of the newsstands and bookstores, along with the names and quantities of the newspapers we distributed. Pilar was a post office employee. She had a voluptuous body and was a little shorter than me. Her round face overflowed with vitality and desire, and her hair was cut short so you could see that her neck still looked the right length.

After exchanging some words to get to know each other at the bar, Pilar said, "This is a beautiful Brazilian song. Will you dance with me?"

"I don't know how to dance," I said. "Do you understand what this song is saying?"

"It doesn't matter," she said. "And don't think that all these dancers know the song lyrics or that they know how to dance. The important thing is to feel the beat. Then you move yourself however you want. There aren't any specific rules. Come on!"

She pulled me by the hand to the middle of the smoky circle of dancers out on the floor. The illuminated disco ball spun over the heads of those who were themselves spinning in place. With her encouragement, I was actually able to shed my reluctance to go out on the dance floor. We spent hours twisting and touching, happy, laughing, lusting after the bodies that pulsed exuberantly around us, and forgetting everything that wasn't before our eyes.

Our bodies were sweating. We kept sipping drinks and frequently went to the bathroom. Naturally, there was no clock on the wall, but when we felt tired, we asked, "What time is it now?"

"Quarter to four," someone replied.

"Let's go then," they said.

In the hallway heading out, Antonio whispered to me, "Take Pilar with you."

"Where?" I said. "When, how, why?"

"Take it easy!" he responded. "Just like that. Just like I said."

"But I—" I started.

He interrupted me, "It was her idea. Just a minute—I'll make her ask you on her own."

He dropped back, getting close to her. Meanwhile, I went out to wait in front of the door. I enjoyed the sweetness of the outdoor air, free from the smoke and the odors. I felt its chill graze my sweaty body.

Mario was next to me, busy kissing Carmen. He leaned her against a lamppost with his hands on her butt, just as he always did even when she was sitting at her secretary's chair in our company. Whenever he kissed her, he reached out to touch her there.

The group all came out, wiping sweat from their foreheads, fixing their clothes, and waving the collars and armpits of their shirts in order to air them out. There was Antonio, Eva, Jesús, Enrique, Maria, and Pilar, who came up to me and said, "How was it? Did you enjoy the evening?"

"Yes," I said.

"Me too!" she said. "There's no more metro service now. I live outside Madrid in Móstoles. How about you?"

"I live here, close by, on Fomento Street. Near Plaza de España," I said.

She said, "Oh, how lucky you are! Do you live alone?"

"Yes," I said.

"Would you let me spend the night at your place?"

"Sure."

We said goodbye to the others, and Antonio said, "Till next time—at work in two hours!" Then he added, with a smile that was meant to be suggestive, "Try to get some sleep, even if it's only one hour . . . ."

We had only turned into the next street when Pilar slipped her arm under mine, clinging to me as she walked. The streets were empty except for people like us, coming out of the clubs, or loitering drunks, who snored in the recessed entryways of banks. From time to time, a car sped past.

Pilar said, "It's lucky that my work is in the evening. This way I'll be able to sleep. What about you?"

"Me?" I said. "I start work at six. So I usually take a nap when I get home. From noon until three, and sometimes until six in the evening."

I could feel her soft breasts against my arm, and her breath on my shoulder when she spoke. She said, "We have clubs in my neighborhood too, of course, but ever since I was fourteen years old I've loved the ones here in the center. I've gotten to know lots of friends in them. How old are you?"

"Thirty. And you?"

"Twenty-six," she said.

We reached the door of the apartment building where I lived and found a cat sleeping there. It got up and moved off when I stopped and took out the key. Pilar said, "Oh, how cute! I have a cat too. Her name is Clara. My friend Laura gave her to me for my birthday two years ago."

I opened the door and turned on the lights in the stairway while she continued to talk about her cat without waiting for an answer, perhaps to fill the silence or to further our acquaintance. "I love her very much, and she always sleeps in my arms. That is, if I don't have another person in bed with me, of course!" She laughed. "Imagine, she gets jealous too!"

We got tired climbing the stairs. Since the stairs were old, like the building, they were made of wood and had high steps that were all the more uncomfortable due to how narrow the stairwell was.

"It's true, she gets jealous of me! Unfortunately, Laura and I quarreled nine months ago. She got jealous over her boyfriend on account of me. How much do we have left?"

"Two floors," I said. "I live on the top floor, the fifth."

Panting, she continued, "Uff! Well, no problem. We're young, and they say that climbing stairs is good for the heart."

She grabbed my arm for help and took off with a jump, moving two steps ahead of me, such that her butt was just in front of my face. It was round and luscious. Her tight black pants revealed its details, and the pants seam sank deep between the two cheeks. The outline of her underwear was visible as a bulge, higher on one side than the other. I knew they were white because I could see the tops of them coming out above her pants. She was bending over as she climbed, causing her shirt to rise a little.

She was breathing hard, but she didn't stop talking: "I live on the third floor, and we have an elevator because the building is new. I own my apartment, which I bought with a mortgage from the bank on the basis of my salary. I've worked in the post office for five years." She stopped at the top of the stairs. "Uff! We made it! Which of the two is it?"

"The door on the right," I said.

She went toward it and stopped, dropping her black purse from her shoulder and leaving me space to open the door. I inserted the key, saying, "It's a small, humble abode. But it is enough for me. I'm comfortable in it. After you."

I turned on the light for her and she pressed ahead down the hallway toward the living room. She gazed at walls covered in the hundreds of pictures that I had cut out of the newspapers. She said, "Oh! It's a museum! Very cozy. Are these pictures from your country? Didn't you tell me you were from Iran?"

"No," I said. "I'm from Iraq."

45

She said, "My aunt's husband is Egyptian. His name is Mansour. He's a nice guy."

She threw her purse on the couch and took off her purple shirt, revealing skin that was as white as the shoulder straps of her camisole. Her breasts looked large, twice as big as Aliya's. The tops of them were bare, and they pushed up the light, silken shirt. I could tell she was not wearing a bra because the nipples were protruding clearly on either side of the deep cleavage, where a small gold cross hung down between the two domes. She began exploring the apartment, sticking her head out the living room door to look it over.

"One bedroom—it's full of pictures too! And this is the bathroom. So, where is the kitchen? Oh, there it is, off the hall."

She headed toward it. I turned on the television, lowering its sound. Then I sat on the chair to take off my shoes. I heard her voice from the kitchen saying, "I feel just a little bit hungry. How about you? Do you want me to prepare a little spaghetti with cheese and milk? An Italian friend taught me that. It's a delicious dish."

"No," I said. "For me, I'll be fine with a couple of dates and a small cup of yogurt."

I joined her in the kitchen. I took down the bag of spaghetti for her, got out a small cooking pot, and lit the stove. She took a glass and used it to carry water from the sink to the pot. Then she came back to break the spaghetti sticks.

She didn't stop chatting and repeatedly passed behind me, brushing her breasts against my back on the pretext of how narrow the space was. Or she'd put her hand gently on my back. She opened the door of the refrigerator and bent over, gazing inside, and half of her back appeared, white under the light, white shirt, while her black pants slid further down with the movement of her buttocks. Even more of her underwear's diaphanous lace was visible, and I could see the fuzz where the line that separated the two cheeks began. Their tops were showing, two round forms extending back and sloping down from her waist on both sides.

She said, "Here's the cheese: yes, it'll work well. And here's a carton of milk." She stretched out her arm with each, setting them on the edge of the stove without taking her head out of the refrigerator. "I don't see that you have any wine. It's true we drank a lot, but I'm dying for one last glass."

"I don't drink alcohol," I told her. "But there is some non-alcoholic beer, if you'd like."

"Where?" she asked, not changing her position.

So I bent over behind her, resting my hand on the bare spot of her back, my face close to hers. I pulled out a can for her from behind the bag of pita bread, and she turned her face and kissed me on the cheek.

"Thanks! Why don't you drink alcohol? Mansour drinks. Are you very religious?"

"No," I said. "Yes. To a certain degree. But I'm not a fanatic."

She said, "I don't believe in the existence of God. But I respect the views of others."

I didn't want to talk more about that subject, which I knew backwards and forwards. Otherwise, I would have asked her about the cross that she wore. I already knew the answer would be along the lines of "It doesn't mean anything. It's a universal, traditional symbol." Or that it was a gift from her mother or her friend. Or because it is beautiful and simple. And further justifications like that, which didn't point to the secret truth of the person's religiosity. At the same time, I had no desire for her to ask me, like everyone else did, about the superficialities of Islam which were the extent of her knowledge: marriage to four women, the veil, the beards, and all those other topics that I had grown tired of debating and explaining, especially when someone you've explained everything to comes back two days later with the very same questions.

"I believe in God," I said, "and I respect the views of others."

She may have sensed my lack of interest in discussing it, so she changed the topic: "You're good at Spanish. How many years have you been here in Spain?"

"About five years," I said.

She kept moving, brushing against me. "And you don't have a fiancée or a girlfriend?"

I said, "Female friends, yes: the co-workers that you saw with us at the club. But no fiancée."

She asked with a seriousness overlaid with humor, "Surely you are married in your own country?"

I responded in a similarly facetious tone, "Yes, four wives and forty children!"

She laughed. Then she covered the pot and said, "Come on, let's sit in the living room for a while until the water boils off, then we'll add the chunks of cheese and some milk. The food is going to be delicious!"

I sat on the couch, and she came and sat next to me, pressing against me and setting her can of beer on the table in front of us after taking two sips. When she saw me staring at the television screen, she said, "There's nothing good on TV now."

True, there were just late night shows advertising different kinds of cars and modern exercise equipment. So I turned it off, and she wrapped her left arm around my neck and reached her right hand to my shirt. She opened the buttons and said, "Why don't you change your clothes? Make yourself at home."

She laughed, pulling me toward her, toward her lips, and we began a long kiss, our tongues, our lips, and our quick breaths intermingling. All the while her hand played with the hair on my chest and moved further down. I had been thinking of her voluptuous breasts since I saw them bouncing in the club. I wanted to know what it was like to touch large breasts like that. With my lips still on hers, I made a move and slid my hand under her light undershirt.

Oh, how nice it was! Soft, my fingers sank into them, and my hands cupped all the way around. I felt both nipples standing erect. My fingertips brushed the ends of them. Then my fingers circled around on all sides. The warm place between the breasts, where they pressed together, made me shudder.

The shudder passed through my body, and my loins tightened. Her fingers descended toward my waist, and she clung to me all the more, melting into me with her eyes closed. I don't know how long we continued like that, but when we stopped and I looked at her face, I found her smiling, blushing. She was even more beautiful with her shining eyes and her deep passion.

I said, "Make yourself at home! You can change your clothes too, if you want."

We went off to the bedroom. I opened a dresser and took out for her a pair of my pajamas. When I turned around, I found that she had taken off her pants. I saw her white underwear pressing into the fullness of her butt and thighs, also white.

"Just the bottoms," she said. "I'll keep this shirt of mine."

I changed clothes too, keeping my back toward her so that she wouldn't see the taut erection in front of me.

We felt comfortable and free, such that she began to move more confidently and spontaneously between the living room, the bathroom, and the kitchen. She brought me back an open cup of yogurt with a small spoon inside. She gave it to me and sat on my lap, filling it up with her butt. I reached around with one hand, which I moved in a circle, caressing it on all sides. She leaned against my chest and kissed me from time to time. I started touching her breasts again, on top of her shirt . . . and underneath.

CHAPTER 5

After considering the matter in a halting, conflicted, and wavering way, I made up my mind not to sleep with Pilar. I would avoid falling into sin that night as far as I was able.

I had never slept with anyone before her. Yet I wouldn't let her know that I was still a virgin because she wouldn't believe me. She would laugh, or she would be afraid, or I don't know what. I was also afraid of God and Grandfather and Aliya. And my confusion, my lack of experience, and the likelihood of failure.

I would be satisfied with the kisses I had won from her and my fondling of her large breasts, which were just the kind that I lusted after whenever I saw such a woman pass by on the street in my daily life. Or when they would bare them in the movies or at the seashore during the summer. For I hadn't experienced anything in my life like Aliya's amazing breasts: neither large nor small, succulent, firm, and erect—even when she was dead. As though they were created precisely to answer my desire. I wanted them that badly. She used to smear them for me with dates, and I would suck them under the poplar trees and the willows, lying on the sand in the middle of the forest along the shores of our Qashmars Village.

Pilar finished eating her meal after giving me a couple of bites to try. It really was delicious. (I said to myself that I would try to prepare it later, which I actually did. I even became an expert with the dish, varying the kinds of cheese and milk.) She washed the dishes in the kitchen, then came out and went into the bathroom. She pushed the door shut without closing it all the way. I heard the tinkle of her peeing. Then she rinsed her mouth, blew her nose, and washed up. She came out, gesturing with her head toward the bedroom.

"Come on."

"No," I said. "I am going to try to sleep a little here on the couch, even if only half an hour. I'm tired, and I usually have a lot of work on Mondays."

Her expression changed a little, and she said, "Why the couch? The bed is big enough for both of us."

"No . . . . Whenever I'm tired, I snore loudly. I also don't want to bother you with my alarm clock."

"Fine," she replied. "Whatever you want." She came over and gave me a kiss on the mouth, saying, "Sleep well."

Then she disappeared into the bedroom. I closed the door after her, turned out the light in the living room, and lay down on the couch.

I wasn't actually very tired because I was used to sleeping during the day. I also wasn't sleepy on account of how hard my heart was beating from having a woman in my house, especially after all those kisses and caresses. I wanted a little time alone to go over everything that had taken place. This always happened with me. After any exciting event or conversation, I would go off by myself for a while to recall it all, contemplating it, enjoying it, scoping out its horizons. My fist squeezed the erection under my pajamas, and Pilar's smell filled the place.

But what had happened brought me back to Aliya. I was always coming back to her, my first and only love story since we were kids in Subh Village. Memories of her fed my deepest desires. She was a cousin on my father's side, and her house was next to ours. We were separated from them by only a low mud wall, which we used to cross by sitting on it and swinging our legs over. Their bread oven was close to ours, so we would gather near our mothers when they baked bread at dawn or sunset. They would talk about the female neighbors, the cows, the chickens, the fields, and the babies while we played around them and took the burnt bread crusts they gave us.

Aliya was my most beloved playmate: I would take her side in all the fights, and I would give her the best of the clay creations I made. Among these was a horse because she loved horses. I painted it white except for its tail, which was black, just like their horse. Her father was the only one in the village who owned a horse—the rest of us only had donkeys—and he called it "Lion" even though it was a horse.

When Aliya got bigger, she began riding her father's Lion. She would shoot off toward the riverbank to let it drink, or she would take it to the field and return with saddlebags full of watermelons and eggplant from her mother. Whenever I saw her passing close by and heading off into the distance, I would remain fixed in place, reliving the scene of her on the white horse, with her long hair, black as its tail, dancing in the wind behind her head like the wings of a happy bird.

My sister Istabraq was our go-between since, as we got older, it became harder to play together or to get away from everyone else for a rendezvous. Subh Village was an open book, filled with prying eyes: everyone knew everything and nothing was hidden from anyone.

When I first told Istabraq that I loved Aliya, she was overjoyed and set off at a run toward our uncle's house. From the window I watched her, the ever skinny and sickly one, as she crossed the mud wall with a single leap and disappeared. Meanwhile, I stayed in my room, trembling. I covered my face with a pillow and squeezed tight. I didn't know what to do, and my heart was beating in a way that I had never known before, except when I was afraid of Grandfather. Istabraq seemed to take forever, but she returned after half an hour, panting, and closed the door behind her. I wasn't able to read anything on her face, but I felt that she carried an answer which would bring me joy or sorrow for the days to come.

She walked around in the room with a deliberate, wicked leisure, interlacing her fingers and cracking her knuckles, one after another. My head followed as she came and went like the pendulum of a wall clock. I grabbed her by the arm when she passed by. I was still sitting on the edge of the bed, too weak to stand because of my trembling.

I was unable to speak, so I asked the question with a choked sigh, "Ahh?"

She gave me a look that held multiple meanings. Then she looked toward the small clay jar that I had made, all on my own, which I had painted with decorative flowers, butterflies, and circles inside circles, like eyes. I considered it the best of my artistic creations, my favorite. For that reason, I had put my pens inside and set it on top of the bookcase near the head of my bed.

"What?" I asked.

Istabraq smiled and pointed her finger at the jar without uttering a word. I understood that she wanted this jar in

54

exchange for speaking. I tried to play dumb to divert her from it, asking, "So? Did you find her?"

Her finger kept pointing insistently at the jar. Without getting up, I reached out my arm and turned the jar over, dumping out the pens onto the top of the bookcase. I held the jar out to Istabraq. She glowed and hugged it to her chest.

"Well? So?" I said, "Tell me, Istabraq! Istabraq, O apple of my eye, God bless you and keep you! You're killing me!"

But she maintained her wicked silence and her insinuating smile. Next, she stretched her hand out to me. I didn't understand. She brought it closer to my mouth, and I knew that she wanted me to kiss it. So I kissed it, but she shook her head and pointed at the ground. Then I remembered that she had been with us for Grandfather's nighttime stories about knights of old coming back victorious from battle, who would kneel down on the ground and kiss the fingers of their beloved.

So that's what I did, looking up from below at her face, which seemed really high up. Then she collapsed onto my face and hugged my head without letting go of the jar. She rained her happiness and her kisses down upon me and cried out, "She loves you too, Saleem! She loves you!"

Thus began my first attempts at writing letters and poetry. I decorated the margins of my letters with butterflies and hearts that had our initials on them and were pierced with arrows. I would sneak into my mother's room when she was away to dab my letters with drops of the perfume my father would bring for her as gifts from his German friends.

In Grandfather's stories about knights, he used to say that they were all passionate lovers and poets. The one he liked most was Antara bin Shaddad, whom he hoped to see in the hereafter because Prophet Muhammad had wanted that too.

55

Like me, Antara also loved a cousin on his father's side, and he would write poetry for her.

In the same way, I wrote my first poems for Aliya. I described myself in them as a brave knight who didn't fear death. I would cut off the heads of a thousand of the enemy's knights with a single blow of my sword. I would wrestle savage lions and crush their heads like eggs in my fist. I would gather stars from the heavens for her and make them into a necklace with the moon in the middle. I would hang this necklace around her neck and force the people to confess that she was the most beautiful woman in all of creation. Likewise, I would expound upon her eyes, even though her eyes were small like the buttonhole slits on shirts, such that her mother used to call her, either playfully or when she was angry, "my little China girl." Nevertheless, I would compare them to two wide, pearly seas, eyes with the majesty of a lion and the delicacy of a gazelle. Her hair was so silky that silk would be jealous. She was the one who taught the branches of trees to sway coquettishly when the wind blew, just like how she walked. Aliya was queen of the world. No one but me saw her crown, yet I would make them see it by the power of my sword!

Istabraq would read our letters when she delivered them. She read my poems, astonished, wishing that Sirat could write poetry like me. As for Aliya, she never mentioned my poems in her letters. I wasn't able to get to be alone with her through all our years in Subh Village, even though I would watch for her day and night from my window. I would intentionally create "chance" encounters in order to exchange a greeting. I would hide myself on the overhanging bank in order to see her when she came to the shore of the river on their horse to let it drink, with her hair flying behind her like the wings of a happy bird. I would see the gleaming of her legs when she waded in the water, the clenching of each buttock when she bent over, scooping up water to drink or to wash her hair. And I was sadder than everyone else when Istabraq's illness got worse and confined her to bed because the letters to and from Aliya were cut off.

I would sit near Istabraq's head, taking her skinny, hot hand between mine, kissing her fingers and crying. I had learned this practice from Grandfather, whose heart would break whenever he saw one of us bedridden. He would sit near our head, caressing our hands and foreheads with extreme tenderness, reciting Qur'anic verses and prayers for healing, interceding with God "as though he saw Him." For that reason, the days when we were sick were the days when we were closest to Grandfather. Whenever we were healthy, we regarded him as extremely awe-inspiring and severe, even though we never saw him hit anyone. But he was more tender toward us than our mothers were when we were sick. So much so, that it sometimes made me long to be sick in order to win the tender caress of his fingers.

Istabraq was my favorite sibling and the closest to me in spirit. She played with me, she organized my room for me, we clipped each other's fingernails, and when Mother was too busy for her, I would help her comb her hair. She would save pieces of dessert for me when I was away, and I would do the same for her. We would share secrets that we wouldn't reveal to the rest of our siblings. I would deliver her love letters to Sirat, and she would take mine to Aliya. Everyone in our family knew of our partiality for each other and the warmth of our love. That was why Grandfather and my father chose me, and only me, to go with them when they decided to take Istabraq to the Kurdish sheikh for treatment. And that was why my heart fell with her as she dropped out of my arms when we first got out of the car in that sheikh's courtyard and we heard the sound of the shot and Grandfather's cry, "God is great!"

Terrified, I fell to my knees beside her head. After looking her over and not seeing any blood, I shook her shoulders and called to her, hoping that she would open her eyes. "Istabraq! My dear Istabraq!"

The Kurdish sheikh came running toward us from the direction of the shot, that is, from the house. He was carrying an old hunting rifle, its muzzle still smoking. He yelled at me, "Leave her, boy! Leave her alone!"

Grandfather repeated the same cry, "Leave her, Saleem!"

I lifted my hands off her without getting up or moving away, watching the two men as they embraced like kids whose team had won a tournament. Both gaunt and with white beards, they were of the same age and the same height. Grandfather was wearing his favorite suit for special occasions, the one we called a zabun, together with the traditional kuffiya headdress. The Kurd was wearing a suit with wide pants. He had wrapped around his waist a sash that matched the cloth of his turban. They couldn't be more elegantly dressed, nor could they be hugging each other any harder.

They patted each other's shoulders and repeated the same phrase: "Oh! My brother and my beloved in God, Mullah Mutlaq!"

"Oh! My brother and my beloved in God, Kaka Hammah."

The Kurd corrected Grandfather, "Actually, I'm no longer Hammah. I've changed my name to Abd al-Shafi, the 'Servant of the Healer,' ever since God poured his blessings upon me."

My father shook his hand, and Grandfather said, "This is my eldest son, Noah." Then Grandfather stroked my head and said, "This is my grandson, Saleem, and his sister, Istabraq."

The sheikh murmured the customary response, "Ah, for God's good will upon you!"

Then the sheikh turned around and called to a girl standing in the door, "Bring me some water!"

She came running toward us in a multicolored dress, like a butterfly, with a gleaming shawl on the top of her head. The sheikh took the small bowl of water from her and asked, "The salt?"

She extended her other fist over his open palm and let the salt stream out of her hand. The sheikh began scattering the salt on the water in the bowl, muttering words we didn't understand, reciting by heart with his eyes closed. Then he spat in the water and continued his enigmatic recitation. Using his index finger as a spoon, he plunged it into the water and stirred like someone stirring the sugar in his glass of tea. He sank his whole hand in the water and began walking around Istabraq's corpse-like body, shaking the moisture off his fingers onto it and reciting, moving around, splashing her with droplets and reciting, until only a little remained in the bottom of the bowl. Then he stopped at her head, opposite me. He bent over and poured it all over her face and cried out with a voice that made me jump, "The all-living God!"

I saw Istabraq open her eyes and look at him. He smiled at her and said, "Welcome, my sweet child!" He straightened up, saying, "Bring her inside."

He went toward Grandfather and put his arm around his shoulders to lead him toward the entrance of the house. My father, the butterfly girl, and I worked together to lift Istabraq up. She took her first steps leaning on me. Then I felt her walk on her own until we made it through the front door, which was a beautiful weave of wood, twisted copper, and colored glass.

The main room was spacious and resembled a mosque, with carpets and comfortable rugs covering the floor. Pillows were piled up on all sides. There were two columns the color of tree trunks in the middle, as well as a coal stove sunk into the wall under a square chimney. Through the chimney came the sound of cooing pigeons that had settled down on top of it in the nest of storks that had migrated. There were many doors in the far walls.

Grandfather and the sheikh sat down next to each other without releasing their intertwined fingers. In the back of the room, there was a bed made with a high pillow and a white sheet, decorated on the edges with flower blossoms. We laid Istabraq out on it, and the girl covered her. I sat at her feet, and my father sat a few feet away.

The sheikh said something to the girl in Kurdish, which we didn't understand, but Grandfather, whose knowledge of that language surprised me, protested, "No, there's no need to prepare food, sheikh! Our road is long, and we want to return before sunset."

The girl paused, seeking further instructions. The sheikh spoke to her in Kurdish again, and off she went, whereupon Grandfather said, "Fine. As you wish."

The sheikh commented, "We have an excellent turkey whose meat is worthy of our distinguished guests."

They let go of each other's hands, and the sheikh patted Grandfather's thigh as he took the conversation in a different direction. "You've lost so much weight! But for my ever-present memory of you and the days we spent fighting alongside our cousin Rashid Ali, I wouldn't have recognized you."

"Diabetes," Grandfather explained, "and the passing years."

The sheikh commented happily, "Ah, too bad! But it's only fair: you've been sucking on sugar your whole life, and now it's time for it to suck on you!"

We all laughed while the sheikh stretched out his hand to Istabraq's forehead. She was looking at us silently, with clear, beautiful eyes. Despite the faint yellow color that tinged their whites, they were gleaming. Their magic surprised me, as though I had never seen them before.

The sheikh said, "She was possessed by a demon, God curse it! It was feeding on her blood, so I killed it."

His words surprised my father and me, while Grandfather replied with the equanimity of one familiar with such things, "God's curse is ever upon Satan and his followers."

The butterfly girl opened a door, out of which came a tumult of voices. She entered carrying a tray filled with glasses of steaming tea. A group of children escaped from the doorway behind her, running noisily, shooting off in the direction of the courtyard to play. She brought the tray around the circle to us, and we took our glasses from it. She smiled at me when she leaned over in front of me, and I smelled her perfume, made from plant stems. When her sleeves pulled back, two white arms like slices of cheese appeared, adorned with delicate gold bracelets and a cheap digital watch.

She bent over the two old men, and the sheikh said to Grandfather, "This is Gulala, my youngest daughter. The last of my litter."

He laughed, and Grandfather commented, "God preserve her!"

Her father asked her, "Where did you put the pen and notebook, my sweet girl?" She gestured with her head to the shelf behind him, speaking some word in Kurdish. He turned and picked up an old notebook. Its paper was yellow, resembling the paper of some of the books there, of which I recognized only the Qur'an. He tore out a sheet and put it on the notebook, which was resting on his thigh. Then he set about writing and asked, "What did you say the name of your daughter was?"

I answered faster than Grandfather, "Istabraq."

He wrote and asked again, "And what is the name of her mother?"

I hesitated because we didn't usually say the names of our mothers: I would always just call her "Mother." So her name didn't come to me as quickly as my name, for example, or those of my siblings. It was the same thing for us with Grandfather's name since we called him "Father" when we were small and "Grandfather" when we grew up, while the others addressed him with "O Mullah!"

Father answered him, "Maryam."

I asked Father in a whisper, "Why her mother's name, and not yours, her father's name?"

Sheikh Abd al-Shafi heard me and answered me from where he was, "On Judgment Day, we will all be called by the names of our mothers because the mother is single and indisputable, while the fathers might be numerous and uncertain." Then the sheikh became engrossed in writing, drawing from time to time upon old books that he pulled from the small shelf behind him.

I glanced at Istabraq and saw her watching Father and me, so I smiled at her. She extended an arm out from under the sheet and beckoned me with the fingers of her outstretched hand. I reached over to her, and she interlaced her fingers through mine. Her palm was warm and radiated tenderness. She closed her eyes for a while before opening them on Father, who had come close to her face to ask in a low voice, "How are you doing, my dear?"

She nodded. He bent over her forehead to plant a light kiss there, then moved away with tears in his eyes.

Grandfather was looking curiously at what his friend was writing, his lips moving as Grandfather followed along. When the sheikh had finished writing, he began to fold the paper in a unique way, doubling it and then redoubling it upon itself until he had made it into the shape of a small triangle, which he closed by pushing a corner between the opening of the folds. He returned the notebook to the shelf and brought out from there a spool of thread. He drew about half a yard of the thread and inserted it through a corner of the triangle. Then he tied the two ends to make a necklace.

He held it out to Istabraq, saying, "Wear this around your neck always, day and night. Do not take it off, except when you are bathing."

While I was helping Istabraq hang the paper necklace around her neck, I heard Grandfather say, "We have a sick cow. Write her a spell too, O sheikh!"

Turning back to get the notebook from behind him, the sheikh said, "At your service! It would be an honor. What's wrong with her?"

Grandfather began describing for him the symptoms of our red cow's illness. After making the cow's necklace, he gave it to Grandfather and said, "May our Lord restore her health!"

After we finished sipping our glasses of tea, the sheikh approached Istabraq. He used his fingers to pull open her eyelids. Staring into her eyes, he said, "There are two small steps left and everything will be finished. Afterward, you'll be a bride as good as new." He yelled toward the far door, "Gulala!"

The butterfly girl approached. He spoke to her in Kurdish. She bent over my sister, and we understood that he

63

wanted Istabraq to be carried to the middle of the square sitting area. So my father and I got up and laid her out on the carpet in the middle. The sheikh went around her, and Gulala arranged Istabraq's dress so that it would cover her nicely. Then she took hold of Istabraq's feet while the sheikh began stretching out her arms along the floor, parallel to her head. He took the fingers of her hands and made them touch each other, calling out to us, "Come over here! See how they are not equal. That's natural: a person is like a car and needs a tune-up from time to time."

The sheikh was both graceful and spry in his movements. Sitting at her head, he stretched out his legs and rested his feet against her shoulders. Then he began pulling hard on Istabraq's arms while comparing her index fingers. Meanwhile, his butterfly girl kept her firm grip on Istabraq's feet. He pulled her more than once, and each time Istabraq closed her eyes but didn't groan.

Then the sheikh called, "Come and look! See how they are equal now. I will adjust you all, for all of us carry minor illnesses. These don't hurt us, but they do add up. Come, my boy!"

He called me over after we had returned Istabraq to the bed, and I stretched myself out in her place on the carpet in the middle. I reached out my arms, and he called to the others, "Look!"

Meanwhile, I was conscious of the butterfly girl's touch on my feet. What was the flavor of her white palms? Her tea had been delicious. The sheikh tugged forcefully on my right arm. He repeated that three times and said, "Finished!"

I sat upright and found myself face-to-face with the girl, who hadn't taken her hands off my feet. "Thank you," I whispered to her. She smiled.

I got up, and Grandfather lay down immediately in my place. The sheikh's attitude made us like kids playing happily. When it was Father's turn, all of us, including Istabraq, laughed to see his huge body and his belly, which lifted his robe in the middle like a tent. I sat right up next to the girl, holding one foot while she held the other. I could smell even more clearly the plant extract perfume that emanated from her.

Grandfather asked his friend, "And how will you pull someone like him?"

The sheikh answered with confidence, "I've pulled some who are fatter than him." When he compared his index fingers, he said, "See how his body is the most balanced of you all. His fingers are nearly equal. He must work a lot. Work is health!"

When we returned to our places, the sheikh directed some words to his daughter. She brought him a small pouch, then headed to the door leading outside and called for the children, who came running. In the meantime, she gathered the empty glasses of tea and went out. The little ones stood before the sheikh in a line. When each child got to the front of the line, he would turn his back to the sheikh, who looked behind his ears. Then the sheikh would bring the child's neck close to Istabraq's eyes, saying, "Look. I've made an incision in the ears of each of them. It's a simple thing. It doesn't hurt, apart from a prick that you'll barely feel. If the wound of any of them were fully healed, I'd cut the ear again in front of you."

Each child went off at a run after showing himself to the surgeon. It seemed that they were used to doing this.

Gulala returned, carrying a copper washbasin and a pitcher of water. She set them down it the middle. Next, she went over to Istabraq and made her sit down. She pulled off Istabraq's shawl and gathered her hair up. She took out Istabraq's silver earrings: crescent moons with a star in the middle, from which other small moons hung down, each of which had a different colored bead in the middle. She examined them, then put them into Istabraq's palm, which was lying in her lap.

The sheikh advised, "Don't lose them while the wound is healing."

He approached her from behind while taking a shaving razor out of his pouch. My heart trembled, and I hoped that Istabraq wouldn't see the razor. She didn't, just as the sheikh intended.

He reached out with the fingers of one hand to fold her ear down. Then he extended the razor blade and made an incision behind the ear, light and quick. He quickly did the same thing with the other ear. At the moment of each cut, Istabraq closed her eyes and only a small squeak came out of her mouth. The sheikh brought his pouch up to her head. Taking a little of the yellow powder inside between his fingertips, he used it to stop up the cuts he had made. Then he took out a matchstick, which he moistened with his tongue and stuck into the pouch. He began applying the powder to Istabraq's eyelids and left them closed when he was done. Then he brought the open packet close to her nose and commanded, "Inhale! Inhale deeply!"

Afterward, he tied up the pouch and put it aside. Gulala turned around to bring the washbasin close to Istabraq's chest. The sheikh said, "There! It's all over. Wash your face and blow your nose. Blow your nose."

Then he returned to his former seat next to Grandfather, explaining the procedure he had performed. "This is for the treatment of Yellowing Disease. I opened her arteries and put in dabagh, a powder from the dried rinds of pomegranates mixed with the powder of seeds from the Glowing Tree. This is a plant found only on the peaks of the Hasarost Mountains.

The fruit it bears are small bells that are heavy with little seeds. Each bell has its own color which gives off light at night. There are seven seeds in each bell, and I pay one lamb per bell to those who go up the mountain. It's a rare tree. Getting there and finding it is an arduous adventure. Yes, its colored bells give off light, like the Christmas trees that Christians have."

Grandfather asked, "And what are those?"

Father volunteered an explanation without looking in Grandfather's eyes, "I've seen them at the homes of my German friends when they are celebrating the last night of the year. It's a tree that they hang colored lights on, as well as paper bells and other things. Gifts and colored socks."

The session calmed down after that. Istabraq's face appeared optimistic and comfortable. We all listened intently to the conversation of the two sheikhs while the aroma of food came to us from a door left ajar. Sheikh Abd al-Shafi spoke at length about the multitude of patients who came to him from all parts of Iraq, as well as from Iran, Turkey, Kuwait, Saudi Arabia, Jordan, and the Syrian deserts. He would treat them and offer them hospitality as his guests, some of them for a couple days, and he wouldn't take anything from them in exchange because, as he said, "this is a gift from God, and he is my reward for it."

Then he counseled Grandfather to treat his diabetes by eating barley bread, reducing his salt consumption, and giving up sugar. "Drink your tea straight, and take a dose of juice pressed from the wormwood tree every day with the morning prayers. It's bitter, very bitter, like the colocynth, but it will do you good, believe me! You'll once again be strong as an ox!"

They carried on a long conversation. The two of them spoke while Father and I were content to listen. They continued to speak freely even around the platter of turkey surrounded by bowls of yogurt. The grilled turkey pieces were arranged in a row on a pile of rice mixed with raisins and various types of spices. They spoke about the tobacco fields and the sunflowers in Kurdistan, about sons and grandsons, about the angels and the Prophet's companions, about the friends they had in common, and about their memories of the days of battle against the English. They cursed the current government.

Following the late afternoon tea, another car stopped in the courtyard of the house, and a Kurdish family of children and an old woman got out. They said that she had been afflicted with the evil eye.

The sheikh said goodbye to us. He and Grandfather embraced, and Grandfather invited him to visit us in our village. The sheikh excused himself, saying that he wouldn't be able to visit because he didn't know when God would send him a sick person whom he was duty bound to treat. "But you, come visit me!"

Grandfather gave him a promise. But he would not be able to keep it.

On the road, Grandfather told us more about the memories he shared with his friend, the sheikh. Istabraq was asking for less water. Father wasn't convinced by what he saw of the treatment, yet he pretended to be satisfied out of deference to Grandfather. All the same, he asked his German friends about it when he returned to Kirkuk. They were dumbfounded and called a friend of theirs, who was a doctor in Berlin. The doctor said, "This treatment for jaundice works too. The powdered pomegranate rinds go through the blood to the worm and drive it out."

My father was reassured. Meanwhile, I was at a loss about how to get my letters to Aliya during the following two days before Istabraq was able to get up.

At least, I was at loss until we found a hiding place for ourselves in the middle of the forest under the willow trees near the shore. We began to call it our nest. It was there that we knew our first kisses and learned what it was like to suck on fingers and lips that were daubed with dates.

CHAPTER 6

I decided to go to my father's club that evening too. I had to find a convenient opportunity to talk to him, or else we could agree on a time to meet. At the very least, I hoped that I would get to know him better.

After coming to this decision, I went over to the kitchen window that looked out on the neighboring building. It had a shabby-looking roof on account of the pigeons having taken over its rain spouts for nests. I had tried so many times to destroy these nests with a broom handle, but they were further back than I could reach. So I just swore at the pigeons. They came from Plaza de la Puerta del Sol in the middle of Madrid and from Plaza de España, where there was a statue of Don Quixote and his sidekick, Sancho Panza. I would sit there and stare at them for a long time whenever my longing for Grandfather and my father grew sharp, as though the two of them were in everything I saw. Meanwhile, the pigeons around me would eat from the palms of the elderly retirees relaxing on the benches. They would eat the tourists' cookies. Then they would come to poop on my clothes, and on the clothes of my

Cuban neighbor below me. What's more, they would even enter the kitchen and poop on my cooking utensils and on top of the refrigerator with the bread crumbs.

When I was with Pilar, she confirmed for me that she had seen them herself. On the morning of the first night that she slept here, just after waking up, a pair of pigeons startled her by taking flight when she first entered the kitchen. She said, "You left the kitchen window open! Why don't you get a cat? I know a shop with beautiful cats. Beeeeautiful! My God, how beautiful they are!"

I had left her that night sleeping in my bed while I passed the time in the darkness, remembering Aliya and our times alone in the hiding place that we discovered in the middle of the thicket, the place that we called our nest. We found it on the second day after we brought Istabraq back from the house of the Kurdish sheikh who had slit her ears. Mother had prevented her from going out, from housework, and from putting in her earrings until she was on the road to recovery. I was walking around, looking for Aliya in order to give her a new poem that I had written for her, along with a letter. I kept passing by their house and didn't see the horse. Then I went among the houses, shacks, and reed huts of the village. I wandered around our Qashmar peninsula, going through the forest toward the shore on every side until I found her on the northern end, closest to the mountain.

She was wading in the water, washing her face. Behind her was the head of the horse, taking a long drink. I got confused, and I hesitated as I thought about getting away or hiding. But she turned and saw me, and the surprise stopped her.

"Oh!" she said. "Hello, Saleem."

She turned around and looked in every direction; I did the same. We didn't see anyone.

I took the carefully folded piece of paper scented with my mother's perfume out of my pocket. I said, "I want to give you a letter. Istabraq can't leave the house. I'd like to talk to you. Are you able?"

"Quick!" she said. "Get into the woods!"

I ran a few yards back and waited at the edge of the forest, keeping my head turned toward her. After waiting until the horse had drunk as much as it wanted, she took a rope out of the saddlebag it was carrying. She put the halter around its head while still turning to look in every direction. She led the horse toward me, its hooves sinking in the sand just as the words which I had prepared in advance sank into the trembling of my heart and were lost. We pressed further into the forest, opening a track for the horse behind us, until we tied it to the trunk of a giant willow tree, where it grazed on the thick grass around it. We explored the area until we found a sandy, circular clearing, shaded by a jumble of poplar branches interlaced in the sky above. There were smaller trees, such as the tamarisk. Reeds went around the clearing, reaching as high as our chests, such that when we sat down on the circle of sand, they were a little higher than us.

We looked at each other. It was the first time that we had been so close. We could hear the racing of our breaths and the beating of our hearts. Aliya asked me how Istabraq was doing, and I began relating to her the details of our journey for her treatment, taking advantage of the narration to regain my voice and my composure. We spoke in low voices that betrayed the pleasure of confiding secrets.

After I finished, I gave her the letter and the poem. I said, "You've never told me what you think of the poems I write for you."

She said, "They are not very precise. Actually, they are one lie after another."

Her words were a shock, and I found myself placing a hand on my heart and swearing to her the truth of my feelings for her.

She didn't let me continue and clarified, "I don't mean that your feelings aren't true. If that were the case, I wouldn't have exchanged letters with you, nor would I have come here with you. What I mean is, your poems aren't convincing because they are filled with lies. You describe yourself as a knight who, for my sake, cuts off a thousand heads with one blow of his sword. In reality, if you actually killed anyone, I wouldn't like you in the least. So this isn't right, Saleem. And you've never seen a sword except for your grandfather's sword that hangs on the front wall in the reception room for guests. Maybe you've never even touched it. What's more, you've never ridden a horse in your life.

"Next, you describe my eyes as being as wide as two lakes, whereas you see that they are small, like the rips that rats make in a dress. Even my mother herself compares me to a Chinese girl, saying, 'Bring me the china tray, my little China girl!' My sister Salwa describes them as something else entirely when she is mad at me . . . ."

"What?" I said.

"No, no!" she said, "I'm too embarrassed to say."

I pleaded with her to tell me. "You must never be embarrassed with me after today."

"Fine," she said. "Salwa says that my eyes are like . . . are like rabbit vaginas!" She said that with a smile, nearly laughing, and I noticed that her small eyes squinted completely to become small lines, which made her even more alluring, like someone beckoning with a wink.

She continued, "Then you say that my walk is what teaches the branches of trees to sway with the wind. You talk about a necklace for me made from stars and the moon, and that I am the mistress of the universe. But I'm just a girl who doesn't know what goes on outside her own village. There are other things too. I'm talking about all these lies, Saleem. There's no need for them. Your letters, with their authenticity and sincerity, are enough to convey your feelings for me."

I felt crushed by the magnitude of this surprise as I contemplated the failure of my efforts and the late nights spent by the light of a candle, squeezing out my soul, tossing and turning in bed as I attempted to compose my poems, which never exceeded a dozen lines. But I sensed Aliya's earnestness, and I saw that she was right. I didn't comment but rather changed the subject to other details of daily life, taking care this time to avoid slipping into embellishments and dreams—despite the unreal quality of our encounter and a feeling that my growing love for her was exactly like a constantly expanding dream.

We agreed to meet daily in this place, which we called our nest. I stood up, extending my hand to help her rise. Her palm was soft like a new pillow. I felt that her touch had a flavor too because it left a sweet trace in my soul unlike any of the other hands I had shaken throughout my life.

I walked with her until we reached her horse. I helped her untie its rope, then accompanied her until she left the thicket in the direction of the shore. She brought the horse to a trot with a quick kick and off she went with a wave to me. I stayed where I was, watching her depart until she went out of sight, her hair flying behind her like the wings of a happy bird. Then I went back to the spot where we had sat together. I lay on my back and recalled the details: her breath, her voice, the touch of her hand, how her eyes closed, and what she had said. The delicious coolness of the sand seeped into my body as I stared up at a pair of pigeons sitting on the intertwined branches with the sky behind them.

When the nearby sun went behind the even closer mountain, twilight pervaded the place. I got up and tidied our nest, smoothing out the sand, breaking the branches that extended into it, arranging the stones around the circular edge. Then I returned home.

I didn't tell Istabraq anything. I was still sobered by what Aliya had said about the lies of my poems. That night, I kept waiting for an opportunity to ask Grandfather about it. I hesitated quite a while, fearing that he'd get angry or rebuke me. It took me a long time to think of the appropriate words to pose the question.

Since I had noticed that his speech never stumbled when reciting poetry, I said, "Grandfather, have you memorized all the poems of Antara?"

"I have memorized many by him and by others," he replied, "but I don't know if I've memorized all his poetry or not."

Then, knowing that Grandfather hated lying and considered it "a scourge worse even than murder because it is the first step on the path of every sin," I asked, "But don't you think that the poems of these knights have many exaggerations? Or even that they come to the point of lying sometimes?"

I expected his reaction would be violent or that he would be silent for a while in thought, as happened with him whenever someone asked him about matters related to Islamic law. But he answered immediately with one sentence: "The sweetest poetry is the most fabulous."

Then he resumed the story he had been narrating that night, leaving me stunned by the force of this second surprise, which was no less than the one caused by Aliya's words.

I wasn't able to comprehend Grandfather's expression very well at the time, but I resolved the matter by abandoning the composition of poetry for good in order to be free of the contradiction that it led me into. And why should I write it if Aliya didn't expect that from me? I read less poetry after that too, and the poetry that I did read from time to time, I began to regard in the light of what both Aliya and Grandfather had said.

I only resumed writing poetry four years ago, here, during moments when a deadly longing for Aliya became unbearable. I wrote a few disconnected fragments. I didn't publish any of them, and I'm not planning to do so now. My childhood dream of becoming a significant poet, or even a professional writer, had dissolved. The three short stories I published in the Iraqi opposition papers in London were only memories of my army days that I composed for myself in order to put them in context or to be done with them. Or else they were a way to use my free time here in an attempt to understand myself more fully.

We began to meet daily in our nest, which became a little wider, cleaner, neater, and more cozy. The rendezvous was usually during the hour of the midday siesta when our families were sleeping. The better we got to know each other, the deeper we fell in love. I brought Aliya my notebook, in which I had taped pictures of actors and actresses. There were also photos of dream-like scenes where I would talk about bringing her. These were pictures in advertisements which I clipped from the German magazines that my father brought, such as a white, wooden house, surrounded by trees and a garden with colorful flowers, sitting on a lake shore with water of the deepest blue. Behind it was a mountain, whose peaks were white domes of snow touching the other white of the clouds.

But Aliya was less affected than I was by dreams. I learned from her to be satisfied and content. I learned a sense of realism and how to find pleasure in working with the simple but real things around us. From her I also learned self-composure and confidence in the present moment.

In my notebook there were other pictures of women with green eyes and blond hair, for whom I would invent names and say that they were international actresses. I pretended to have a wide knowledge of the world's celebrities despite never in my life having set foot in a movie theater up to that point.

Because we could think only of each other and would hurry to our rendezvous, we would get up from the family table before eating our fill. I would take a handful of dates with me, wrapping them up in a piece of paper that I would push into my pocket. Aliya was like me, Grandfather, and the majority of the Mutlaq clan: she loved dates. The first time, when the handful of dates was gone, we kept our sticky hands raised in the air, delaying our descent to the shore. I don't know how, but I got hold of her hand and began sucking her fingers. She liked the idea and grabbed my fingers in turn to suck on them. At first, she laughed. Then we gave in to a delicious daze of obscure shudders which drew our lips together without our hands slipping away from each other's fingers.

That was the first and sweetest kiss of my life. Aliya's lips were delicate, like the rest of her body, the details of which I began to discover later on. Her body was soft and firm at the same time. Not soft like butter, but rather like fresh cheese. Her lips combined the flavors of date and human. I discovered only then that even humans have a particular taste, just as every fruit or creature does.

After the first kiss, we were silent for a long time, staring at each other, shaken up and afraid. For the rest of the meeting, we communicated with our glances, not uttering a single word. We got up and went to the shore, where we washed our hands and faces. After that, she left and I stayed behind alone, as usual. I didn't return to the nest but stayed on the shore, throwing stones far out in the middle of the river. Then, just as my father used to do, I sat on a rock and hung my feet into the water until the sun set. With a grave expression, I recalled the taste of the kisses and feared God.

I fell asleep late that night after tossing and turning in bed for a long time. I awoke before sunrise, sweaty and terrified from a dream in which I saw myself in the fires of hell. I also saw the angels of hell, whose gigantic size and cruelty Grandfather had described. They were heating iron with which they seared my lips. There was a fearsome sizzle, and the smoke rose up, together with the smell of grilled flesh. Meanwhile, I sensed the presence of God, who was supervising my punishment as it was meted out, watching from a high place that I couldn't see. The voice of Grandfather was ringing out angrily, "He deserves it! I warned them all! O God, my God, I told them! O God, my God, bear witness!"

I pushed off the covers and looked around. Smoke was rising along with the smell of my mother's bread from the oven at the edge of the courtyard. I jumped up and hurried over to sate my thirst from the jar I had left by the door. I drank a lot of water, but it wasn't enough. I felt the dryness of my lips and a stinging sensation.

During our meeting the next day, I hesitated for a long time before kissing Aliya because hell was on my mind, accompanied by Grandfather's voice and the gaze of God. But I couldn't resist the temptation of that pleasure. So I decided to ignore those other things, to put off thinking of them, deciding that this sin of mine wasn't serious like adultery. I justified it to myself, saying, "The sweetness of kissing Aliya in this world is worth the pain of my lips being seared in the world to come."

We began to spend less time talking because we spent most of our time kissing. I loved her. It was as though I were "in a lofty (aliya) garden in which no babbling is heard." Our hands reached out to the other's back, butt, neck, hair, and the curve of the shoulder. But Aliya pushed my hands away the first time they moved down to her chest toward the alluring bulge of her two nipples, which looked like chickpeas lifting up the thin material of her dress.

"It's wrong," she said.

"But we are going to get married," I said. "Aren't we going to get married?"

Her face lit up, and she hugged me tight. Then she gave my hand freedom to slip down the front of her dress, and we stretched out on the sand. Later on, she offered herself to me entirely. I loved her completely, as though I were "in a lofty (aliya) garden, where grapes hang low."

She would reserve the ripest dates to the end of our meal, which grew more elaborate with bread, cucumbers, and figs. She would open the date with her teeth and remove the pit to throw into the thicket. Then she would pass the hollow date around her fingers like a ring before offering me the fingers to suck. I saw her close her small eyes, turning them into two lines with projecting eyelashes, just as they looked whenever she laughed or smiled widely.

Sometimes she would leave the date-ring on her finger for me to eat off before I sucked the finger, and sometimes she would eat it, when the date wouldn't stay fixed to her finger. After the fingers, she would smear her lips with the next date as though she were putting on lipstick. She would then smear mine and push the date into my mouth, and we would give ourselves over to a long, gentle sucking of each other's lips.

Aliya had a light fuzz on her top lip, which only two kinds of people saw: those who loved her and those who hated her. The lover, myself, saw in it the consummation of her beauty and, later on, a way to preserve the nectar of dates so that our kissing lasted longer. As for anyone who hated Aliya, he would take the fuzz to be a blemish to be harped upon because there was no other fault to be seen in her body. It was just like the matter of her small eyes. I came to love them precisely for how small they were and the way they disappeared into her face when she laughed or surrendered to the pleasure of our caresses.

After a while, when Istabraq was regaining her strength, she asked me about my letters. I told her about the nest where Aliya and I met, without indicating its location. I said that we left our letters to each other there when it was impossible to meet. We would put them in an agreed-upon cleft at the bottom of a tree trunk rising on the edge of the nest, against which Aliya would sometimes lean, or under white stones we had designated.

"Istabraq," I said, "please don't ever tell anyone about this!"

"Don't worry," she said, as her mouth gaped open in astonishment. Perhaps she and Sirat also made their own special nest because she began disappearing from the house whenever she found an opportunity.

Later, Aliya began opening the buttons on the top of her dress or taking it off entirely. Then she would smear her breasts with the juice of dates and lie back in the sand, closing her eyes and letting me lick them, suck them, love them as she moaned and trembled. That is what made me always look at a woman's breasts afterward. Aliya had ideal breasts, neither too big nor too small. Each one was only a little larger than my cupped hand, and its nipple would stand up under my tongue.

Aliya was like Grandfather and me in her passion for dates, but she loved the river more than I did. The intensity of her love for it is what made me first love it too. But I began to feel jealous later on because of how much she would talk about it when it flowed in front of us. She imagined the river more beautiful than I saw it to be. Afterward, my relationship with the river became a mix of enmity and intimacy when Aliya, at the end of that summer of ours, drowned there.

I had once asked her not to go too far out in the water when she was swimming.

"Don't be afraid," she replied. "It's my friend."

She used to say, "Life is a beautiful gift from God, Saleem. It is not for us to object about how big or long it is. Rather, we receive it with gratitude and enjoyment."

That's why I thank God whenever I remember Aliya, and I blame life for taking from me the most beautiful gift it gave, for taking Aliya from me. I blame the river. I hurl rocks, and I cry. Then I throw myself into its embrace, wishing that it would take me to her.

It took her from me on the night of the festival, when we all went down to the riverbank. The families gathered on the shore where the sand and the pebbles came together. They spread out their sheets on the ground, and the mothers arranged dishes of food and sweets made the night before. The children played, running around the groups of adults, with the mountain echoing back their cries. The fathers tended the fires and grilled the meat. Tears caused by the smoke mixed with tears caused by laughter. We all swam in the river in specified areas not far away: the men in one part and the women—without taking off their dresses—in another. Only the children had the freedom to cross between the two areas, pleading with the adults to teach them how to swim. Grandfather kept repeating the Prophet's traditional command, "Teach your children archery, swimming, and horseback riding."

He was alone there in the middle, up on a low hill, sitting on the one chair he owned and watching everybody. My father had brought this chair for him from Kirkuk when diabetes had eaten away at his body so much that his bones jutted out, such that sitting directly on carpets would hurt his back and his pelvic bone. For that reason, he kept with him a square, spongy pillow that he would use as a cushion wherever he sat, including on that chair, the only one in the village. It provoked everyone's amazement because it would fold up. We felt how light it was when one of us carried it, walking behind Grandfather to the place he wanted. My father said the Germans had many kinds of chairs, and this kind was used for nude sunbathing.

All the mothers brought samples of their specialties to Grandfather, but he ate only a little and distributed the rest to the children who came up to him. All of us young men were stealing glances to the women's area, hunting for glimpses of dresses clinging to bodies in order to meditate upon the image afterward when we secretly jerked off. Some of us were going especially far out into the river or being creative in our jumps to attract the gaze of the young women.

Suddenly, a cry went up from the women's area. "Aliya! Where's Aliya? She dove and didn't come up! Aliya is taking too long to come up!"

We all ran over there, mingling together. The women had all come out of the water and stood in a row on shore, pale, terrified, pointing to the place where Aliya last dove. Her mother was screaming the loudest, crying out and beating her breast. Yet of all those present, my heart was the most anguished.

All of us men threw ourselves into the place where the women had come out and where the fingers were pointing. I dove as deep as I could and opened my eyes, not caring about the strands of seaweed that got into them. For a wide expanse, I only saw rocks at the bottom. I didn't come up until I was about to suffocate. I pushed off the bottom with my feet and shot upward, thrusting my head to the surface. I gulped the air, panting rapidly, sweeping my gaze to those around me in case anyone had found her. Then I dove before my lungs had gotten their fill of air. Those were tense, bitter minutes. A nightmare of minutes, days, years. A nightmare lasting a lifetime.

My father caught hold of me when he noticed me stumbling about nearby, about to pass out. I was vomiting up the water I had swallowed. He lifted me in his strong arms and pulled me to shore, scolding me all the while. There were women's legs standing around me in a circle, and Mother dropped down next to me, wiping the water and the snot from my face with the hem of her dress. Meanwhile, I pulled my face away from her hands so as not to lose sight of the search. My chest rose and fell with the speed of my breathing and the drumming of my heart. Mother pressed down on my arms to prevent me from getting up again.

Moved by compassion, Istabraq approached from behind me. She draped a towel over my shoulders and embraced me. Her hands dried my shoulders with calming caresses filled with compassion. I felt her trembling. Then she exploded into tears and fell on me, her arms around me, when we all saw one of the men raising Aliya's body to the surface. My hands came to my face, but I didn't turn my eyes away. I wasn't able to get up.

The lament echoed back from the mountain even louder than it had gone out. The swimmers circled around the man carrying her. One of them pulled down Aliya's dress to cover her legs as the one carrying her approached us. She was sleeping in his arms as the water dripped off of her. Her arms hung down, as did her long hair, the ends of which were the last to take leave of the river. Even when her hair broke free, it stayed connected by a thread of water, making her hair look like her horse's tail when she would wash it. It wasn't like the wings of a happy bird, flying behind her head when she shot off on the horse.

They came toward us. Aliya was sleeping meekly in the arms of the man bearing her. She rained down on the river from every side. Everything about her pointed down to the water—her feet, her arms, her fingers, her hair, her dress— everything except her breasts, which rose up just like I knew them. Two domes, their details revealed by the wet dress. That was the last that I saw of her before she disappeared behind the surrounding bodies.

They brought her to where Grandfather was sitting and laid her out there in front of him on top of the soft pebbles, waiting for what he would advise them to do. Everyone withdrew up there, and the surface of the river cleared. I was not strong enough to stand. My head fell between my knees. I wrapped it in my arms and broke out in sobs, weeping. Istabraq embraced me from behind, and our tears shook us together, while Mother hugged me to her chest, kissed my head and said, "I know, Saleem. I know everything."

Mother never said anything else about my love for Aliya after this, but she would look at me with pitying eyes and a broken heart.

Istabraq became closer to me in the following days. With compassion, she frequently consoled me and shared my tears,

84

alone together in my closed bedroom or at the shore. She sometimes came with me during my secret visits to Aliya's grave. It sat alone at the foot of the mountain before being transferred later to a larger graveyard for our village's departed. Istabraq helped me search for white pebbles to arrange on the grave, and she cleaned the two stones marking it.

Istabraq confessed, "I was the one who told Mother about your relationship. She was so happy, and she said that Aliya's mother was happy too. They agreed to pave the way for your wedding to take place at the next festival."

I didn't find any letters from Aliya in the cleft of the tree trunk in our nest, against which she used to lean her back, offering to me her breasts smeared with dates. I didn't find a letter under the white stones. And I never returned to the nest after my last visit, when I found that someone had taken a shit in the middle. Our nest was no longer a secret, as long as someone had seen fit to take a shit there.

The sight of Aliya sleeping, her body raining down on the river, was the last I saw of her. Her breasts, alive in the midst of death — it's the most vivid of all my images of her. I always have it with me. It was my close friend, along with dates, in those moments when I burned with desire for her.

Only twice did I call it up when masturbating in secret. Once when I was in the army, stationed at the three-way border between Iraq, Turkey, and Syria, on the bank of the Khabur River. It was after my guard duty on a long night, during which Aliya had been my only companion. I yearned for her. I yearned to touch her. Her image diffused a warmth and a sweet trembling in my veins.

I went down to the river after turning over the watch to the next soldier. The moon was radiant, bathing the entire sky and all of creation with glorious silver light. I left my rifle on the shore. I took my clothes off and put them on top of it, next to my shoes, and I slipped quietly into the river. I reached my hand under the water to my taut erection. I closed my eyes on the memory of Aliya and the scene of her domed breasts under her last wet dress, and I began to stroke and stroke. I stroked until the climax of desire and pleasure. Afterward, I felt empty, ashamed, and guilty for what I had done with her when she was dead. And I wept.

I resolved never to repeat what I had done. But I did repeat it four years ago when Pilar was sleeping in my bed after an orgy of our kissing and my caressing her breasts. After I sensed that Pilar had fallen asleep, with her perfume filling the apartment and me stretched out on the couch in the living room, I felt the erection under my pajamas, and I remembered Aliya. There was still half an hour before I had to leave for my job distributing newspapers.

I got up and went into the bathroom. I closed the door cautiously behind me, taking care not to make any noise. I filled the tub with water and quietly stretched out in it. I reached my hand under the water to my taut erection. I closed my eyes on the memory of Aliya and the scene of her domed breasts under her last wet dress, and I began to stroke and stroke. I stroked until the climax of desire and pleasure. Afterward, I felt empty, ashamed, and guilty for what I had done with her when she was dead. And I wept.

I hurried to wash up. I put on my work clothes and ate a couple of dates with a mouthful of cold milk. Then I went out, leaving Pilar in my bed and lighting a cigarette as soon as I passed through the door of the building.

When I reached the office, I found Antonio sitting in the truck, smoking as he waited for me. He had already finished bundling and loading the newspapers we had to deliver. I sat behind the steering wheel next to him and turned the ignition. We set off as usual, with me driving. He slapped my right thigh and said in a significant tone, "I knew you'd arrive late . . . . So, how was your night?"

"Perfect," I said. "But I left her sleeping in my apartment."

"Don't worry," he said. "Pilar's a good girl. I've known her a long time. By the way, she's especially attracted to foreigners. Her last boyfriend was Italian."

I gathered my laundry from the clothesline. Remembering what Pilar had said, I made sure to close the kitchen window so the pigeons wouldn't get in. I had resolved to go to my father's club that night. Pronouncing the Arabic words badly that morning, Rosa had said tonight's party would be beautiful. But that isn't what impelled me to go. Rather, it was my father. I had to find a chance to talk to him, or else we could pick a time to meet. My new father who had emerged, just like that, in my life here. As surprising as a head bursting out of the water after being submerged for a long time. I wondered whether my father still remembered the evening of the festival when Aliya drowned. Did he still remember her like I did after all these years?

CHAPTER 7

I arrived at the club at a quarter to midnight in order to beat the rush. As with every other club, the dancing started after one o'clock and would continue until the first rays of dawn appeared to dispel the dark.

Club Qashmars was in Veneras Street, on the left-hand side as you approach (as I always did) from Plaza de Santo Domingo. It was in the basement of an old building, and it may have been used as a storage basement at first and during the days of the Spanish Civil War. But at some point along the way, a door leading to the narrow street had been put in. The space was initially used as a shop for selling drinks, then later as a club after my father and his girlfriend, Rosa, had leased it and renovated it for that purpose. Across from the club, on the right-hand side of the street, was a shop owned by a Chinese family who sold groceries, nuts, soft drinks, and cigarettes until very late at night, which they could do because the family lived in the back section of the store.

The outer door of the club was black and made of wood. I found a young woman crying in front of it. Her boyfriend was trying to make things right. He kissed her, but she pushed him away gently and wiped her eyes. They were standing exactly in front of the handwritten phrases on the door. When I reached for the door handle, they moved a little out of the way.

After the wooden door, another door followed, made of an iron grate. It was open and chained to the wall. Then a stairway went down about seven feet, with a turn in the middle. It was covered with a dark red carpet, though it had become nearly black from absorbing smoke and from the multitude of shoes passing over it. That smoke, together with the din of the music, was the first thing that struck me when I opened the black, wooden door. Next was the noise of conversation and laughter rising up to me. I recognized Rosa's laugh, then my father's, after I heard someone yell "cabrón," which is Spanish for "asshole." When I descended the last step, I found them standing around the bar. As it was, there weren't more than fifteen people there, all of them gathered around my father, with glasses in their hands and laughing.

Fatima was in her permanent spot behind the bar, near the cash register. As soon as my father saw me, he called to me extravagantly and led me over to the group. He introduced me to those who were standing there with a theatrical gesture: "Saleem. This is Saleem." Then he proceeded with their names, pointing at each of them and putting his finger on their chests, including the girls, for whom he would set his finger between their breasts or even on them, taking it away quickly with a comic motion, making them all laugh. There were Germans, Dutch, Austrians, and Spaniards. As for the last one, who was short and fat, he said, "This is Jesús, the cabrón," and they all burst out laughing.

He didn't tell them that I was his son, but rather "Saleem." Just "Saleem." Then, when I stood next to him, he wrapped his arm around my shoulders to demonstrate for them the intimacy of our relationship.

Rosa asked me, "Anything to drink?"

"Nothing, thanks," I said. "Not now. I'll order something for myself in a bit."

My father was speaking with some of them in German, others in English. With the Spaniards he spoke a limited number of words, most of them curses. But whenever necessary, he got help from Fatima to translate, or from Rosa, with whom he spoke three languages: German, English, and a bit of Arabic. He held a glass in one hand and a cigarette in the other. Nevertheless, he never stopped using his hands while speaking, waving them around. He would often wrap the arm which ended in a cigarette around the necks of the others. But once he discarded the cigarette, his fingers would grab wherever they landed, pinching the skin of those standing around him, who were intoxicated by his noisy presence.

New customers kept arriving, coming down across the black entryway with its red carpet, which looked like an outstretched tongue. It was like an open mouth vomiting out people, each of whom came to the circle around my father and started joking with him. Their circle grew larger and more crowded, and because most of them knew each other, little by little I found myself alone on the edge of the circle. I didn't know anybody, and I didn't find a way in. I felt incapable of joining in their jokes and matching their noisy laughter. So I took myself quietly away toward the bar and sat on a stool between the beer taps and the cash register, opposite the place where Fatima would always stand. I greeted her, and she smiled sweetly. Her hands didn't stop wiping the glasses with a towel tied to the edge of the white work apron hanging from her neck like a cook's apron.

"What would you like: German beer or Spanish beer?" she asked.

"Neither," I replied. "I don't drink beer or any alcoholic drinks. I'll take a Diet Coke."

"You really don't drink?! Oh my God, that's great!" She showed her surprise, but I didn't know how serious she was being.

"And you?"

"I don't drink alcohol either. And if I sometimes have to, to be polite, I'll drink a non-alcoholic beer."

"How long have you been in Spain?" I asked.

"About four years."

"And how long have you worked here?"

"For six months, ever since it opened."

"How? I mean, how did you find this job?"

She leaned her head back and laughed, trading a dry glass for a wet one to wipe. "It was a coincidence. Or luck. I'm not sure which. I was passing by one morning, and I went into the Chinese shop across the way—do you know it? I wanted to buy some notebooks, pens, and so on. You know, school supplies for my sister. She's young, fourteen years old, and I want her to finish school and not drop out like I did."

As the number of people coming in increased, so did the empty glasses that the other workers brought to Fatima from all corners of the club. They would also carry back orders. Fatima stopped talking with me in order to converse with them, taking the empties they brought back and pouring drinks to send out with them. I took advantage of the pause in our conversation to sip a little Coke and to observe Fatima more closely. I also looked around at the surroundings, over to where my father was hidden behind the crowd. I could only see his head with its colorful braid and hear him laughing. It resounded loudly and was echoed all around by the laughter of the others, interspersed with curses in every language.

"The important thing," Fatima resumed, "is that I found your friend, Mr. Noah, there. He was looking for things for the final renovations: screws, nails, brackets, shelves, and things like that. He bumped into me inside the shop and immediately said in Arabic, 'Excuse me!' I answered him in Arabic, 'No problem!' So he said to me, 'You're an Arab!' And he began to ask me the Spanish names of the things that he wanted, which I helped him with. I stayed with him to translate until he had finished paying, and then he said, 'Do you want a job?' 'Yes,' I replied, 'but in what?' He led me here, where the decorators were just about to put on the finishing touches. And so it was that we began talking it over until we came to an agreement. But the surprising thing, which you might not believe, lies in the condition he imposed on me before we sealed the deal. Excuse me for just a minute."

A customer, perhaps Dutch, came up to her and ordered a cocktail. Given that he didn't know what the drink was called in Spanish, she asked him if he could speak French. He said yes, and they began talking in French until she had made his drink and he went away, thanking her.

She came back over to me with a sweet smile on her face that was obviously connected with what she would tell me: "The condition he gave was that I memorize the entire Cow Sura from the Qur'an before he would sign my contract!"

I was shaken by surprise, and as I heard my father's laughter booming out, I asked, "Seriously?!"

"I swear to God Almighty! He gave me a copy of the Qur'an. I too was as surprised as you are."

"Huh! And then what happened?"

"I took the Qur'an and told him to give me a week."

The crowd in the club was getting bigger, and four people came up to ask Fatima for drinks. At the same time, one of the waitresses brought in additional orders. Rosa came over and asked Fatima whether she needed someone to help her. She said no at first and then changed her mind after another customer came up with her boyfriend. I think it was the one who had been crying at the door when I came in. At Rosa's command, one of the waitresses went around the far end of the bar to join Fatima.

Rosa approached me and patted my shoulder in a friendly way. She said in the manner of a professional maître d', "So, how is everything?"

"Fine, thank you."

"Look at him! He's as happy as can be."

"Yes, yes, I see him. Rather, barely: I only see his braid and hear the roar of his laughter."

She laughed then herself and went away to some other business. From all this, I realized that her role was to supervise things in general, and my father's was to socialize with the clientele. Fatima's job was to watch the cash register and to prepare glasses and drinks, with help from of one of the waitresses if it became very busy.

Fatima smiled at me whenever she approached the register. I was sitting in front of it and leaning my arm against the edge. When there were only two customers left, the other girl took their order, and Fatima stood in front of me. She kept on working: recording the receipts, drying glasses, and preparing small dishes of olives and chips.

I asked her, "And what happened?"

"Naturally, I agreed. It was the opportunity that I had been waiting for. I would obtain a good contract for a stable job after having spent the previous years without a work contract, moving from cleaning houses, to caring for children and the elderly, to working in immigrant restaurants."

"And you memorized the entire Cow Sura?"

"Yes! I went home and locked myself in like a student getting ready for her graduation exams. Before that, I had only memorized the short suras of the Qur'an. My sister helped me memorize it, though at the same time she laughed at me. She thought that I was like her, studying all over again. To a certain degree I found this condition strange, but it also gave me confidence in Mr. Noah."

"Do you still have it memorized?"

"I do. Because he tests me on it at the end of every month before he hands over my salary, and he deducts one euro from me for every mistake. At the same time, he gives me a bonus of fifty euros on my salary if I don't make any mistakes. That was our deal. He tests me without a book since he has the entire Qur'an memorized."

My eyes just bulged since I couldn't find anything to say in reply. I felt a revival in my obscure hope that my father was, deep down, just as I knew him to be. At the same time, I became even more confused and surprised at this entirely different person that I saw in him now.

"And what about the rest of the women working here? Did he give them any conditions?"

"No, of course not. They are Spaniards and Christians, so it's entirely different. Rosa is the one who picked them. I'm the only one that Mr. Noah hired. He was also taking me as his translator, as he put it to Rosa. And Rosa does not refuse his requests. She is madly in love with him. She says that she has never known a man like him in her life. Actually, I too have

never known a man like him—with the strength of his personality, his big heart, his intelligence, and his vitality. You are also
from his village in Iraq?"

"Yes . . . . Yes."

"I like Iraqis. All of us Moroccans like Iraqis."

Then she went away to help the other girl. I stayed where I
was, lighting one cigarette after another, sipping the Coke, and
observing what went on around me. The noise increased as
the club became more crowded with young people of various
nationalities and lifestyles. I didn't understand how hippies,
tourists, blonds, blacks, immigrants, homosexuals, and racist
skinheads all came together. Everyone was submersed in a
cloud of smoke while the disco ball oscillated on the ceiling
above the performance stage. The members of a Brazilian band
mounted the stage and began taking their places with their
musical instruments, checking them over. The dark-skinned
singer adjusted her bra straps and tested the microphone.

My father went up and got the party going with a comic
monologue in a mix of languages, with Rosa sometimes translating. He joked throughout with some of the people standing
nearby, and there was laughter and applause. Then the place
ignited with Samba songs. The dancing bodies undulated,
shaken by the drums, which were struck by a dark-skinned,
muscle-bound percussionist dripping with sweat. Sometimes
he bit his lip in concentration; other times he would let out
a frenzied cry, which animated the gyrations of the dancers
even more.

I looked at my watch and saw the hour hand pointing at
2:00 a.m. I looked at Fatima and saw her moving quickly. She
nearly flew from one side to another, filling orders like a bee
going about its work lightly and skillfully. She never ceased to

smile, despite the flood of noise that forced us to bring our faces close together and shout when we were talking.

I asked her, "How is it that all these radically different people come together in one place?"

She laughed and said, "Everyone asks the same question. It's your friend, Noah. Because he does that, some of them call him president or teacher. Some of them call him the messiah since he brings together the wolf and the lamb and makes peace between them. But he refuses such titles and only goes by his own name, which some think suits him even better, given that the original Noah brought together all the different kinds of creatures into his single ark. According to Rosa, he loves his name very much and says that God is the one who chose it for him."

Suddenly, like a scene from a comedy, a violent commotion arose between two customers in the middle of the dance floor just when we were talking about his ability to reconcile the incompatible. An empty beer bottle flew through the air from that direction and shattered against the fingers of Fatima's right hand, which had been holding the top of a tap, pouring a beer for someone. She cried out, and her blood mixed with the drink in the glass she was filling.

The music stopped and my father burst out of the crowd, coming over to Fatima to comfort her and check her wound. There was a cut that ran along the back of her four fingers.

"I'm sorry," he said to her. "It will be okay."

He told me to put pressure on the wound and take care of her. Then he went back to the adversaries and raised his voice above everyone else's in a rebuke. With the help of some others, he separated the adversaries and sat them down away from each other. The whole time he was cursing and scolding them amid everyone's silence.

During this time, I went behind the bar with Fatima. I took hold of her bleeding hand, washed it, and comforted her. She had actually calmed down already, though the surprise had frightened her a little. I began to dry her hand with the apron, which she had hurried to take off. I saw the size of her chest for the first time. It was small, but the two breasts were firm, set apart, and upright, like the newly developed breasts of a young woman. Rosa brought me gauze and a bandage, together with a bottle of iodine, which she had taken from a small first-aid box that was hanging in one of the dark corners. I sat Fatima down on a nearby chair and began wrapping her hand, going around the fingers on their own, then all together.

My father angrily mounted the stage. In a style that ranged from serious to joking, he began addressing the assembly over the microphone, reminding them of the rules of the establishment and his rejection of violence in all its forms. After I had finished bandaging Fatima's hand, I put my hand on her shoulder, and she stood up with me. We began to watch my father, who was speaking at that moment, giving his address in English, which he would translate himself into German, while Rosa next to him would translate it into Spanish.

"This is a place for happiness, for coexistence, for tolerance, for getting to know each other, for love, for peace, for dancing, for life, for kissing." (He kissed Rosa, and the crowd laughed.) "For the pleasure of caressing bodies and asses." (He reached a hand over to Rosa's butt, and they laughed and clapped.) "Violence is forbidden here, along with arrogance, racism, and calls for force and heroic deeds. Whoever among you wants violence, chivalry, and empty heroism, here's my passport!" (He took his passport from his pocket and held it up.) "Let him take it and go to Iraq. I guarantee he'll find violence there. They'll teach him manners, they'll put some muscles on his bones, and he'll eat the shit he's looking for!"

Laughter and applause went up. He came down and reconciled the two adversaries, making them embrace each other and apologize. Then, to the one who had thrown the bottle that injured Fatima's fingers, he indicated that he should apologize to her. A fat German came toward us and began apologizing to Fatima.

My father said to him from behind, "Kiss her hand, you donkey! Just like respectable men do to respectable ladies."

The guy did so, smiling, and Fatima smiled while extending her hand. Everyone applauded, and my father called out to the music band, "Come, now! Let's continue the party!"

The din and the dancing started up all over again. Then my father came back to Fatima and embraced her, saying, "My dear Fatumi, how are you?"

He examined her wrapped hand, and she said, "No, it's nothing, just a light wound."

He said to her, "You can go home, or to my place, or even to Saleem's, if you want."

"No," she said. "I'm fine. I can stay here and take care of the receipts at least."

"Fine, just as you like. In that case, have a seat. And whenever you feel pain or want to leave, just go."

Then he spanked her on the butt and disappeared again into the middle of the crowd, his laughter rising above the noise.

I said to Fatima, "Where do you live?"

"In the Barajas district, near the airport."

"And how do you get there every night then?"

"Sometimes I take a taxi, and if it's late, I take the subway when the first train comes at six."

"And Mr. Noah's house?"

"It's close to here, on the next street over."

"In any case, if you want to go to your house, his house, or even my house, I'm happy to walk you there."

"No, thanks. I'm fine."

I came out from behind the bar and sat back down in my place in front of her. After about an hour, I noticed that the atmosphere had come back to normal. The dancing and the drinking continued, and Fatima resumed punching in the receipts with her right hand, the smile never leaving her face. I wrote my address down for her on a paper napkin I took from the dispenser in front of me. Then I said goodbye to her and headed off for home.

CHAPTER 8

I couldn't fall asleep until very late. I stayed up smoking and recalling what had happened, what I had learned that day about my father. So, he still had the Qur'an memorized. And he was proud to confess Grandfather's method of naming in our family, which he considered to be names chosen for us by God.

He had made Fatima memorize the Cow Sura, yet he spanked her whenever she passed by him. And it was he who had raged like a bull and turned our entire life upside down on account of a guy grabbing my sister Istabraq's butt.

He took charge of this incompatible multitude, yet he, throughout his life, left the management of our family, and even of his very self, to Grandfather. He would obey Grandfather without discussion, without even looking him in the eyes.

He now drank wine voraciously, yet he was the one who never left a prayer, a fast, or any religious duty unfulfilled. He lived with Rosa, and she wasn't his wife. (And how exactly did he live with her after what the electric torture had done to his testicles?) His mouth poured out the coarsest of curses in all languages, yet he was the one who never uttered an offensive word in his life. He laughed the loudest of all those assembled, yet if he used to laugh, it wouldn't be more than a smile because "if the upright believer laughs, he must not guffaw."

I was thinking that there were two people inside my father. The person that he revealed back there was hiding here; the person that he revealed here was hiding back there. But he didn't abandon either of them for good. Sometimes he injected one of them into the other.

And finally, what about the way Grandfather died!?

It had been Grandfather's dream to construct what might be called "The Ideal City," or at least "The Ideal Village." The clash with the government furnished a suitable opportunity to put this dream into effect. To a large degree, he succeeded during the first two years after we moved. It was an ideal place for isolation: a peninsula that the river encircled on three sides, with the mountain on the fourth. He made the mosque the center of the village and the biggest, most important, and most beautiful of its buildings, even though it was just a large hall with a prayer niche. He attached to it a small room and a bathroom. He fashioned the shelves of its library by himself out of branches from willow and tamarisk trees, stacking all his books on them. He didn't have more than fifty books, most of them containing religious or historical material or popular legends. In their entirety, they formed the sum of my first reading: I read them all as I had a lot of free time during those years.

Perhaps the best explanation for the absence of any delay on Grandfather's part in choosing the place and deciding to move there is that, over the years, he used to stand and gaze for long periods out the window of our guest room in Subh Village. Perhaps he was forming this plan.

Grandfather's insistence on accepting the insulting name in the beginning, and his promise to change the name to Dignity after we took revenge, was a tactical, premeditated step. It demonstrated his intention to establish a goal that we needed to struggle to achieve. Tying the goal to the name of the village meant we would always remember it. At the time he had said, "Let the Prophet be our model in everything, for he is the one that changed the name of the city Yathrib to 'Medina, the Illuminated City' after emigrating there to establish the core of the Islamic state, which would stretch to all corners of the earth after he was gone. When we avenge our dignity, we, too, will name this village of ours Freedmen, The Absolute, or Dignity."

That was then. And till this day, I haven't liked those names because of how diluted those generalized, traditional concepts have become. What's more, deep down I preferred the name Qashmars, at least from the point of view of how pretty the sound was to pronounce. Perhaps my father was of the same opinion, seeing that he had bestowed upon his club here that very name.

In the first two years after our move, we noticed a new-found vigor in Grandfather's body and mind. What's more, there was even an improvement in his health, so much so that he was usually not content just to give orders and plans (even the architecture!) and to oversee the work, but he found it hard to keep his hands from taking part.

He used to say, "This will be a good town, with the Qur'an as its constitution and sharia as its legal system. We will make it a model of virtue and an earthly base from which people depart for heavenly paradise!"

In the village, Grandfather filled the role of absolute governor. No details escaped his notice. Leaning upon his Pakistani cane, he shouldered his almost eighty years and made daily rounds in the village: writing marriage contracts and blessing those who married young, determining the punishment for wrongdoers, and reconciling adversaries. He would visit the sick, and he would recite incantations and Qur'anic texts over the places of their injuries. He would censure the women who revealed their legs when sitting in front of the washtubs and call to account whoever among them overburdened their donkey. He would proffer advice and teach both young and old about their religion and their world. He meddled in everything and exercised control over everything, doing it all out of zeal to apply "God's statutes" in their entirety.

He made the mosque's prayer hall, which was next to our house, his dwelling place and a headquarters for administering all village affairs. Prayers, meetings, and religious celebrations took place there. There, too, were the judgment council, conversations, colloquies, and worship. There was the school where we all learned. And there were the books, the box of sweets, the bag of dates, the poison for rats, and the hereditary family sword.

When picking the muezzin, who performed the call to prayer, he chose the darkest and strongest person among us, thereby imitating Prophet Muhammad's choice of Bilal the Ethiopian. And because he didn't want to change the man's name, he commanded the muezzin to name his son Bilal. Then he called him "Abu Bilal," that is, Father of Bilal. Actually, he did this even before the son who would confer this name upon the father was born. He ordered stairs to be built that would lift Abu Bilal to the roof to recite his call to prayer from there. So we all woke up at dawn to his voice, which became more beautiful with the passage of time and Grandfather's instruction. In the same way, we would measure the time according to his five calls to prayer. Meanwhile, Grandfather reserved the Friday call to prayer for my father, perhaps with the intention of forcing him to come back every weekend from his job in Kirkuk.

My father was the only one who left the village, so he became, in this way, our sole link to the outside world. And judging by the intensity of my father's obedience to Grandfather, I was certain that he would have left his job, which he loved, had Grandfather asked that of him.

Grandfather stipulated that my father take a path across the mountain and not through Subh. So in order to cross to the other side of the mountain and reach the highway that connected Mosul and Baghdad, my father followed a trail made by the livestock. He would flag down cars going in the direction of Mosul, and from there to Kirkuk. He would sometimes travel by foot, taking more than an hour to cross the mountain. Other times, one of us would accompany him on a donkey. I was the one who liked doing this the most because my father would talk to me on the road about the outside world and about the Germans, whom he liked a lot. He would say, "They really like eating sweets, and they have many different kinds. Next time, I'll bring you a piece of their chocolate. They are like our family, which is obsessed with dates, but their sweets have an infinite number of colors and flavors."

Along those lines, I also remember him talking one time about German women. He was talking freely, as though he were alone, or—who knows?—he may have meant to inspire a sense of friendship and treat me like a man. "Their hair is like a field of wheat at harvest time. The fuzz on their breasts and their pubic hair is like a handful of golden grass. But their smell! Their butts are their least beautiful parts since they are not rounded at all, but just a continuation of their backs and thighs. Butts without personality! If they would encircle their green eyes in the middle of those golden faces with black eyeliner, it would be amazingly beautiful—amazing! Their breasts are large and swaying. Faces and bodies as smooth as butter, but bland and boring—is it because butter is eaten with sweet things rather than savory? There are lots of fat ones with huge bodies. Tall ones, some of them reaching as high as that tree—that one, do you see it? Yes, I'm serious! They are less talkative than the other foreigners I know. Somewhat cold. Is this what makes them love the sun? In the sun, they become red like tomatoes."

He would talk to me about other foreigners, whom I would imagine to be tribes like us—French, Thais, Americans, and Indians. Also the English, about whom he would say, "I don't like them because they have yellow smiles."

I wondered to myself at the time about the secret behind his hatred of the English because of their yellow smiles while at the same time he loved the Germans, who had yellow hair. But I quickly gave up wondering since I didn't understand what it meant to have a yellow smile, and I didn't want to interrupt his fiery discourse about the Germans: "There in Germany, Saleem, everything an Arab longs for exists in abundance. I mean water, plants, and attractive faces. All of Germany is one big green field. Do you understand what I'm saying? It's true they might be so serious as to be dry in their interactions, as though they live for work alone. They are stubborn, like your grandfather, and for that reason, iron suits them. They use it to make the best cars. They are very successful in iron and music. A challenge strengthens them, and therefore they built their country up quickly after the war, surpassing their enemies in construction. They have freedom there. Everybody says what he wants and does what he wants, without anybody interfering in his choices. Freedom, Saleem. Ah, freedom! Do you understand what I'm saying, Saleem?"

"Yes, Father," I said, even though I was picturing his words in my own way more than really understanding what he meant. As far as I was concerned, these were startling images, like the ones Grandfather etched in our imaginations about paradise. I mixed my father's descriptions into Grandfather's until they seemed the same to me. The only difference was that what my father described was present on earth while what Grandfather described was found in heaven.

When the donkey went up the mountain, my father would put me in front of him so that his enormous body wouldn't lean on my small one. And during the descent, he would set me behind him so that I would lean against his back. The moments when I would wrap my arms around his chest and embrace him were my favorite of all since I felt so close to my father, as though I were at one with him. I felt a wonderful tenderness, trust, and warmth because these were the times of my closest contact with him. I felt a great love for him, and I felt his love for me. As though he were the one embracing me and not the other way around.

When we got to the highway, he would get down and take his bag out of the saddlebag and then say, "As you well know, God's satisfaction comes from the satisfaction of parents. I am satisfied with you, Saleem, no matter what you do. But you must try hard to please Grandfather and your mother too, okay?"

I would nod my head in agreement and murmur, "Dad, don't forget—"

Smiling, he would cut me off, "Yes, I know. I'll bring you the glossy German magazines. Don't worry."

Without taking me down from the donkey, he would wrap his arms around me and kiss me. These were the only times that he would kiss me, for he would absolutely never do that in the presence of anyone because Grandfather rejected an indulgent upbringing for boys.

"Go, now. Goodbye, Saleem."

I'd pull on the donkey's rope to turn it around. "Goodbye, Dad."

As I got further away, I would keep turning back toward him until he had gotten into one of the cars. If we were still close enough to see each other, he would wave to me from the car window, and I would wave back. I would keep watching the car as it got further away until it became a small dot moving along the black line of the road and disappeared. Afterward, heading back home along the same path, I would think about him and the glossy German magazines he'd bring for me. I would cut out the pictures and glue them in my notebook to show to Aliya, promising her a dream similar to those pictures.

My relationship with my father was one of emotion and spirit while my relationship with Grandfather was one of intellect and rules. I wasn't different from any of the other children in Qashmars Village with regard to my feelings and my total adherence to the system that Grandfather created for us and bound us to. Especially since that system was comfortable and successful in the first two years. At that time, contentment and harmony prevailed in the lives of everyone. Our most joyous moment was the Friday prayers, when we would all gather together, young and old, the males forming the front rows with the women in rows behind them. We would wear our best clothes and put on perfume. In the spring, we would spread our prayer mats on the pebbles and sand outside the mosque, and Grandfather would stand in front of us, using the external stairs as an elevated platform to preach to us. We felt our complete unity, our brotherhood, the purity of our spirits, and our closeness both to the sky and to God. When our "Allahu akbar!" pealed out during the prayer and we uttered "Amen!" in unison, our voices resounded together with the lapping of the river's waves and the rustling of the trees, producing a distant echo from the foot of the mountain. Such moments filled us with a mythical awe, similar to what we imagined for the day of resurrection.

Those were the moments when we were most unified, most at peace, and most spiritually pure. We truly felt that we shared one spirit. On the intellectual and conceptual level, we felt complete concord. It was as though we had one shared mind, with which we thought, or which would think for us. Was this not Grandfather himself?

He would undoubtedly have realized his dream of an ideal village, had not the roar of bulldozers surprised us one morning on the top of the mountain. They were plowing a wide road toward our village, following the course of my father's small footpath. The government came along this road with their officials and their power lines. They gave us televisions and built a school for us out of concrete. All Grandfather's efforts to prevent these things met with failure, and he became all the more sad, angry, and emaciated.

The war on the Iranian front intensified, so the government sought additional young men and adults from all corners of Iraq for the draft. Grandfather's health collapsed even more as he saw the further failure of his dream. He vomited blood when he learned that the government had recorded our village in its official papers under the name of Faris Village, meaning 'knight' and referring to the dictator. For that reason,

Grandfather resumed his emphasis in subsequent Friday ser-
mons on our holding on to the name of Qashmars until the day
we avenged our dignity, the day when we would exchange that
name for the awaited name, such as Freedmen.

The front against Grandfather grew wider. Nevertheless,
he didn't stop fighting what he was up against, and his strongest means was his sermon after the Friday prayers: "Television
is the devil in your homes. It will corrupt your women against
you! It is the one-eyed Antichrist spoken of in the Qur'an.
That's why it has only one eye! The government school teaches
your sons unbelief and godlessness. The police are the dogs
of the tyrant. The war against the Muslim nation of Iran is
an aggression that God does not accept. This is a hard time,
when holding fast to your religion is like grasping a live coal.
Be patient! Hold fast to your religion however much the burning coal of your times sears you. For that is easier to bear than
entering the tormenting fire in the hereafter and remaining in
hell for all eternity!"

But the people feared the government's violence more
than they feared Grandfather's threats, which were postponed
until the world to come. Thus, even though the people in the
village still showed him deference and obedience, the threads
of control began to slip from Grandfather's fingers.

The government was able to conduct a new census of us
after they came with a police force that outnumbered us and
was better armed. They issued us new identity cards, omitting
the nickname Qashmar as well as our old surname, leaving
us in their records with just our first names and our fathers'
names. After they established the number of young men and
adults fit for military service, they ordered them to join the
army. The men refrained, however, after a vengeful sermon

from Grandfather. Therefore, the government decided upon a sudden nighttime raid to seize them one by one. So Sheikh Mullah Mutlaq prepared them to resist and distributed the men—armed with rifles, pistols, multi-pronged fishing spears, axes, clubs, and knives—out on the roofs of the houses, in the ditches between them, in the middle of the thickets, and behind the boulders at the foot of the mountain.

On that night, which would have led to ruin and a real massacre, my father got credit for saving the village when he managed to cut the electricity at the main converter in the center of the village. This made the government give up on their night assault on the village. They came by day to the houses, one by one. The men were then forced to go willingly with the police in order to avoid being shamed in front of their women and children.

Grandfather had no remaining stratagem. He could only promise imminent relief and insist that the people be patient. As a response to what had happened, he increased the frequency of his lessons with the children at the mosque, competing with and correcting what the government school was attempting to teach them. He kept on in this way until the decisive blow came and utterly crushed his spirit.

That was the day when, a little before sunset, a convoy of government cars came, like red ants, crawling down the black road's switchbacks. It stopped in the middle of the village, and seventeen coffins wrapped in flags were lowered to the ground. These coffins contained the corpses of the young men of the village who had been killed in the latest attack on the front. Among them were Ahmad, Fandi, Salih, Nasser, Qays, Hasan, Jamal, Mahmoud, Mudhi, Khayrallah, Abdallah, Sirat (my sister Istabraq's beloved), and my brother Hakeem. They put them down and departed, disappearing up the foot of the mountain in their convoy of cars. They left our village with the blackest night, stricken with bitter lament. The women tore the flags because they needed to tear something out of anguish for the dead, especially after Grandfather forbade them from rending their garments. The village square around the coffins was transformed into a scene of weeping hell.

Grandfather sat silently on his chair, suppressing his tears until midnight, when sorrow burst the dam of his endurance. He exploded in tears and fell down unconscious. We carried him to his bed in the corner of the mosque. There, after we had splashed cold water on his face and sliced an onion under his nostrils, he revived a little and ordered the men huddled in a circle around him not to bury the corpses this time until they had been avenged. Then he drifted away, sinking into his final stupor.

For a whole week, the corpses were rotting. Their odor spread everywhere despite the efforts of the women, who sprinkled them with perfume and piled bouquets of flowers on the coffins. The men returned to where Grandfather was laid out, repeating their request for permission to bury the corpses. Given that he knew better than they did, none of them dared remind him that Islam stipulated speedy burials for the dead. Nevertheless, and without opening his eyes, he refused with a shake of the head.

No longer able to bear the odor and the people's anguish, our village morphed into a suffocating nightmare. Conversations between people dropped off. Silence reigned, except for the wailing of women. Children stopped playing and were content to pass their free time wandering about aimlessly, staring. My father didn't go to work. Instead, he remained beside

Grandfather, washing him before every prayer and turning his face toward Mecca. He saw Grandfather praying with his eyes. At least, he saw Grandfather's closed eyelids flicker and his lips move. That was when—after spending the final days wandering about, visiting Aliya's grave, our nest, and the shore where she drowned—I decided to leave.

I wasn't able to sleep the night I made the decision. I tossed and turned in my bed. Then I got up, wandered out around the village, and came back to the house. In the end, when the night was hastening toward dawn, I resolved to inform my father and then go. I set off in the direction of the mosque's main hall because he was sleeping there beside Grandfather. As soon as I passed near the window, I heard his voice in a fierce debate. I stopped and looked in the window, but I wasn't able to see anything because of the shadows. Nevertheless, I remained nailed in place, trembling to hear my father's voice with this strange tone for the first time in my life. His voice was powerful and confident, as though rupturing all inhibitions, and it contained a bitter reproach. He directed his words toward Grandfather, whom I didn't hear make any response.

My father was actually shouting in Grandfather's face, if they were in fact face-to-face in this darkness. I heard the following words, which were strained by tears and anger: "Father, put aside your loftiness and your arrogance. Ease just a little the weight of your righteousness upon us. As the Qur'an says, *You will not tear open the earth, nor will you reach the height of the mountains.* You will not fix the world by yourself. The world will not be as you want it, nor as anyone else wants it. Stop looking down on our weakness, for we are mortals and rotting corpses. Have mercy on our weakness, on our situation and our mistakes.

"Father, as far as I'm concerned, you are a god, or else the Lord's agent here on earth in front of me. But I am a mortal ruled by his limitations, and mortals rebel against their gods in moments of weakness or moments of strength.

"Father, I'm choking from your chains around my neck. I can no longer endure your commands and prohibitions. My spirit takes strength from being bound to you, but it longs to breathe freely, far from your control.

"Father, sometimes I love you in a way that surpasses my love for myself. But at other times, I wish you were dead.

"Father, I'm speaking to you in the dark because I am unable to see you. I have never looked you in the eyes my entire life, and nevertheless, they are more real to me than my own eyes. I see through the eyes of no one but you, even though I haven't looked at them. My own eyes long to exist on their own before they rot away. Our corpses are rotting, Father! Have mercy on our weakness. You are leading us to ruin!"

As dawn was breaking, I began to see my father leaning over Grandfather's body, their faces close together, and his hands on Grandfather's chest or to either side of it. I found myself shaking on account of what I had seen and heard. I hurried to leave, returning to my bed. I was trembling and uncertain as to whether I was asleep or awake. Sweat drenched me, and my throat was dry. I curled up in a fetal position under the covers, and I began to open and close my eyes in the shadows, listening to the beating of my heart and the racing of my breath.

Then I heard my mother start wailing and crying out, "The mullah is dead!"

My father gave the call for the dawn prayer from the roof of the mosque.

I got up and packed as many of my belongings as I could fit into my bag. Then I hurriedly slipped over to the bed in the next room where Istabraq was lying, sick with sorrow over the loss of Sirat. I whispered to her, "My dear Istabraq, I can't stand it here any longer. I'm going to leave the village. I'm going to leave the entire country. I'm leaving everything here behind, and I don't know where I'm going or how. I'm going anywhere but here, and I don't know when I'll come back. But the one thing that I know is that I can't stand it here for a single moment longer. I'm choking! I'm choking to death!"

CHAPTER 9

I woke to someone ringing the bell from the main door. I looked at the alarm clock next to my head and saw that it was quarter to six in the morning. I got up and went over to the receiver for the door phone. "Yes, who is it?" I asked.

A voice came to me: "It's me, Fatima. I'm sorry to disturb you, but I need to talk to you. It's urgent."

"Oh! Fatima. Come on up. Come on up! I'm on the fifth floor."

I left the door open and heard her steps coming up the bottom flights of the staircase. Meanwhile, I hurried to the bathroom, washed my face, rinsed my mouth, and quickly combed my hair. Then I hurried to clear off the surface of the coffee table, which was cluttered with an ashtray filled with cigarette butts and date pits, empty yogurt cups, and scattered newspapers. Afterward, I went to the door and stood waiting for her as the sound of her steps approached the top.

She was panting on account of the climb, and I repeated the playful cliché that I had learned from Pilar and shared with everyone winded by the climb to my apartment: "It's good exercise. They say that climbing stairs is good for the heart."

I reached out my hand, taking hold of hers and helping her up the last two steps.

Smiling, she said, "Good morning!" Then she added, "And what am I going to do with a strong heart if I have no intention of shipping it off to compete in the Olympics?"

We laughed together, and I led her inside. Traces of fatigue from staying up all night were clearly visible on her face. Little red veins stained the whites of her eyes. I noticed that her hair was long and pretty. When she passed under the lamp hanging in the hallway, I saw that the skin of her face was tired and shining as though smeared with oil. I led her to a seat in the living room, and she flopped down, heaving a powerful sigh, or as the saying goes, the uttermost sigh of her heart.

Like everyone who comes to my house, she too began to stare at the pictures of Iraq which covered the walls. She said, "This is the first time I've seen a house like this. Are they pictures of Iraq?"

"Yes," I said. "I put them up with the hope of reducing my sense of exile. But they actually increased it."

She said it was a lovely idea and that she wanted to examine every single picture another time because she loved Iraq and didn't know much about it. She was wearing a simple dress, which made her seem more feminine in my eyes since in my long years here I had only seen a few women who weren't wearing pants.

I asked her if she wanted to eat or drink anything, and she requested just a little water. I brought her a glass and sat in front of her, asking about her injured hand.

"It's certainly better," she said, "but it still stings. I need to replace the bandage. Do you have any here?"

"Yes," I said, getting up. "I have iodine and bandages."

"No, not now," she said. "Please, sit. I came to tell you what happened. You have to talk to Mr. Noah. I think he needs a close friend to understand and help him."

"What happened?"

"An hour ago, at the end of the party, he quarreled with Rosa. She was furious and left in tears for Barcelona."

"Why?"

"Mr. Noah drank more than he should have last night and got drunk. He joked more with the customers. He danced and flirted more with the girls, kissing a few of them sometimes. Rosa was consumed by jealousy. She restrained her anger until the end of the night, when the battle between them began. He answered her harshly, and she picked up her purse and went off, leaving him staggering around drunkenly. I tried to calm her down but couldn't. Then a co-worker and I took Mr. Noah home. We left him on his bed, passed out like a dead man. He slept in his clothes just as he was. I took off his shoes. Then I locked up, leaving the club in a disastrous mess, and came to you."

"Does this happen often?"

"No, not like this. He drinks, but he never loses consciousness or his self-control. He drank so much yesterday and became drunk like never before. I didn't know what to do, so I tried to think of someone else who could help me with this situation. But although Mr. Noah has lots of acquaintances, I noticed that he and Rosa harbor a special respect and affection for you. What's more, you're from his village, his country, his culture, and you speak his language, so I thought that you would be the best person to talk to him, listen to him, understand him. In any case, you're his friend, right?"

117

I bowed my head for a few moments, thinking the matter over and deciding how to respond. I sighed audibly, then looked at her and said, "He's my father."

The sudden surprise threw Fatima back in the couch. Her eyes widened, and all the features of her face changed. Her mouth gaped open, and she hurried to cover it with her right hand. "Really?"

Without any further details, I confirmed that it was true, and I told her that she had to take it easy, to sleep. Likewise, that we ought to let him sleep, and after a few hours we would go to him. She said her body was exhausted, but that her mind was awake, and she didn't think she would be able to sleep. But she needed to shower and change her bandage. Then she had to call her sister to set her mind at ease and let her know that she wouldn't be coming home that day. So I told her, "Sleep a little now, and then we'll take care of everything."

She said, "Half an hour should be enough."

I led her to my bed in the bedroom and took out a pair of my pajamas for her, but she insisted on sleeping in her dress just as she was.

I closed the door on her and went down to pick up bread, cheese, and milk. Then I began preparing breakfast for both of us. This time I made it rich and varied, adding eggs, olives, and jam, since it wouldn't be appropriate to offer her the traditional breakfast I have every day: coffee with milk, cookies, and cigarettes.

She slept more than an hour, and I heard her gentle snoring, like that of an overweight child exhausted from playing or whose nose was stuffed up.

I spread newspaper out on the coffee table, as usual, and started bringing in the dishes and arranging them. Then I got the coffee machine ready and started it before heading to the bathroom for a shower. When I finished and came back out, I found Fatima sitting in the living room. I greeted her, my hands still drying my hair with the towel.

"Good morning! Did you sleep well?"

"Yes," she said. She smiled and added with a feminine shyness, "Did I bother you with my snoring? I snore when I'm tired."

"No! Your snoring is really light compared to mine. I'm the smoker. Mine's like the roar of a tractor stuck in the mud."

She laughed, and I showed her the way to the bathroom door. Meanwhile, I went into the bedroom to change clothes. I noticed that she had made my bed in an elegant way, different from how I always did it. I felt that each of us—the bed and I—smiled, giving the other a meaningful wink. I took all the medical bandages and iodine I had out of one of the dresser drawers and carried them into the living room. I brought in the coffee, and I put a popular Fairuz cassette that I was addicted to listening to every morning into the tape player. I sat smoking and waiting for Fatima to come out.

The bathroom door opened, and Fatima's head and half a naked shoulder appeared from behind the door frame. Her hair hung down, dripping wet. The sight startled me by reminding me of Aliya when she swam—or when she drowned. Before this idea could distract me entirely, she said with a happy smile, "Oh my God! I love Fairuz so much!" Then she asked, "Do you have another towel, or should I just use the one in here?"

I jumped up. "I'm sorry! I forgot. Of course, I do." And I quickly brought her another towel, which she took with a naked arm that gave off the scent of woman and soap. She thanked me and smiled, then shut the door.

I turned up the volume of the Fairuz song. Then I sat smoking another cigarette and waiting for Fatima while my heart became more and more tender, like butter melting in a dish of warm oil.

We finished our breakfast, during which I asked, "Did you try the dates?"

She replied, "I only like them during Ramadan."

That provoked a twinge of disappointment, and I said, "Try them; they are Iraqi dates."

"Really?" She immediately took one.

Fairuz finished her set of songs. The scent of Fatima's body mixed with the fragrance of the soap filled the room. She said to the cigarette I held out, "No, thanks; I don't smoke."

I began to ask her about herself. I noticed that she told her story confidently, on account of feeling relaxed and comfortable. Little by little, with the gradual progress of the morning light, she shared her story and her personality with me.

Fatima was from Tangier. She was four years younger than me, and she'd been living in Madrid for four years. She had four siblings (and for what it's worth, she likes the number four). Her two older sisters were married; she and her younger sister were here.

As for their only brother, he drowned in the Strait of Gibraltar during a risky crossing to Spain on one of the "death boats." He had been forced to drop out of college without finishing his degree after their father was laid off from his restaurant job. That job had lasted more than thirty years, but when the restaurant's owner died, his sons converted it into an arcade. With the change, they replaced the entire staff with younger workers. They gave her father a little severance pay, no longer needing his services. He rapidly aged and various illnesses crept into his body. Fatima's brother took on several jobs in an effort to meet the family's living expenses and the cost of their father's treatment, but these wore him down and he couldn't make ends meet. So he decided to embark upon the adventure in which he drowned. He had spoken to them about the dream of Europe and all the money he would send back to them.

In the face of her parents' distress and her father's condition, Fatima dropped out too. She went from one job to another in shoe and fabric factories and then a clothing workshop. Still, they went to sleep most nights without dinner. For that reason, she didn't hesitate in agreeing to marry a man from their street. He proposed when he came to visit his family after a long sojourn in Spain. Fatima moved with him to Spain, carrying with her the unrealized dream of her brother. But after two and a half months, she discovered her husband's alcohol addiction and his laziness. He would beat her, and he would squander the money she earned from cleaning rich people's houses. So she separated from him, and then they were divorced. Fatima began to send her family what extra money she had. Later, she brought her younger sister to Spain so that she could keep her company and fulfill the family's dream that one of them would finish school.

I sensed in the depths of her tone a touch of firm self-confidence. There was also a cloak of sorrow that Fatima endured with a certain matter-of-factness drawn from the repetition of her daily routine. She had achieved a certain contented acceptance. Indeed, by recalling this sadness throughout her daily life, she had transformed it into a source of strength, and from there, she developed a certain pride in herself. There was something in Fatima the Moroccan, I don't know what, that reminded me at times of Gulala the Kurd.

I don't know how the conversation brought us back again to my father, but I found an appropriate way to ask why she tolerated my father's flirtations. To be more precise, I wanted to know about his touching her butt, something that preoccupied me deeply. She laughed, her eyes gazing happily off into the distance, like someone cherishing a memory. She began trying to explain to me her feelings toward my father, in whom she had found the father figure she needed. She sought in him an image of her own father: he made her memorize verses of the Qur'an; he gave her orders at work; he showed a special trust in her and handed over the cash register to her; he gave her a set of the keys to the club and his house; he needed her for translating; they understood each other on account of being from the same culture in the midst of people from many different cultures; he sought her help to understand many things in his new environment; he inquired about her sister and her parents; and he compensated her well.

"And the spanking, Fatima! I'm asking about how he keeps spanking your butt!"

"Oh!" Even this pleased her since that was what her father used to do too. When she would go to him as a little girl to show him her drawings or carrying her school report card, he would lift her to his knees, hug her to his chest, kiss her, and give her some dirhams to buy anything she wanted. Then he would set her down between his knees, spank her lightly on her bum, and say, "Run to your mother in the kitchen and tell her how well you did!"

It is not at all uncommon for people to feel a familiarity and intimacy after only one or two meetings, just as though they have known each other for a long time. That's exactly what happened between Fatima and me, a fact that we remarked upon during our conversation on the short walk to the club. For me, this was the first time that I had felt the oppressive feeling of exile lightened. The fact that we were speaking in Arabic had a big role in that.

Fatima was also closer to what I imagined a woman to be, or how I grew up understanding them. She seemed somewhat like a sister or a mother. She acquiesced to the role bestowed upon her by life and her environment, the particular time and place in which she lived, together with its framework of traditional concepts that inspired confidence, composure, and an acceptance of reality. There was a sense of adapting oneself to the situation, without relinquishing an ethos of putting things in order and making improvements.

Our instinctive use of many religious phrases as we spoke made us feel a greater trust and closeness. Before we had left, when she saw my prayer rug hanging behind the living room door, in the one spot without pictures, she asked me, "Do you pray?" Without a doubt, she already knew the answer.

"Yes," I said.

"Me, too, as much as I can. I'm fully dedicated only during the month of Ramadan . . . . I prefer people who believe in God."

We arrived. She took out a bunch of keys from her purse and opened the door of the club. We plunged in, going down the stairs after she had turned on some of its dim lights with a small button behind the panel of the door. As soon as we reached the last step, Fatima illuminated the club by pressing a button near the entrance to the bathroom, and the big overhead lights went on, revealing a chaos that resembled a veritable battlefield where hostilities had just ceased. The floor was covered with paper napkins, cigarettes, and all the detritus of the night's festivities. Overturned chairs, empty or half-empty glasses and bottles were scattered in every direction. There were cigarette butts everywhere, along with lemon peels and olive pits, more cigarette butts, dishes, ashtrays filled with cigarette butts and toothpicks, empty cigarette boxes, and the remains of half-eaten sandwiches, potato chips, yet more cigarette butts, and the putrid odor of nicotine dominating the place.

I said in a stupor, "What is this dump?"

Fatima said, "This is how it is after every night."

"What's to be done?"

She smiled, rolling up her sleeves and tying on her apron, and said, "I'll get to work cleaning it."

"But this is a lot for you to do by yourself. Especially when your hand is injured!"

"It's not a bad wound. And you'll see how I can make the place spick-and-span within one hour."

"Can I help you?"

"No. It's my job, and I know how to do it. You go to Mr. Noah."

"What time is it now?"

"Ten-thirty."

She headed over to her purse and took out a bunch of keys once again, which she began to explain for me: "This is the key for the building's main door. It's the one here around the corner to the left. And this is the apartment key, on the third floor. Letter C, which is the one in the middle, with its door exactly opposite the elevator."

I remained fixed in place for a moment. It was as though I were wavering between my desire to seize this opportunity to be alone with my father, for which I had been waiting so long, and my reluctance and even fear of being alone with him. Or was my wish to remain in Fatima's company the strongest?

I saw her still standing there, leaning on her broom and watching me as though waiting for me to leave. So I left.

CHAPTER 10

I stood in front of the door to my father's apartment, filled with uncertainty. My heart and my breath were both racing. I strained my ears to hear what was going on behind the door. Nothing. Just silence. Should I ring the doorbell? Should I pound on the door with my fist? Should I steal away and escape? Or should I just open the door and go in? Perhaps that was the very reason Fatima had given me the key. But how could I enter a house unannounced? That was not something I had done since leaving our home in the village. Yet wasn't this my father's house too?

I knocked on the door with the backs of my fingers, a light knock that I scarcely heard myself. Perhaps it was just an excuse so that I could say without lying, should I be asked, that I had knocked. I waited a little; then I inserted the key and turned it slowly. I pushed the door carefully, as slowly and quietly as I could, like someone opening an ancient chest. I entered with silent steps and closed the door as quietly as I had opened it. There was only silence, broken by my father's snoring in some corner.

The living room was twice as big as the one in my apartment. In the wall opposite the door was a window that looked over a narrow courtyard between the neighboring buildings. There were four other doors. One was closed. Of the three that were open, there was the kitchen, the bathroom, and the snoring of my father, which must have been the bedroom.

I approached and saw him lying in bed, on his stomach, in his socks and his clothes from the previous night's concert. I had never before seen my father or anyone in our village sleeping on his stomach that way. I remembered the time Grandfather angrily scolded me when he saw me stretched out like that on a rug in his large sitting room. He had yelled, "Get up! Get out of that position! Don't ever stretch out on the ground like this again. It's a wicked way to lie down."

I don't remember who it was that explained the matter to me afterward. Whoever it was had said, "That's because the earth is our mother. It isn't right for us to stretch out upon her in this way, like a man having sex with his wife."

I advanced with steps so slow and quiet that I almost got cramps in my legs. I sat on the couch that presided over the living room, under the window looking out on the center courtyard. I started looking the place over in the sunlight pouring through the window.

Lying there on the coffee table in front of me, beside an ashtray and some German newspapers, were my father's keys. I knew them from the familiar key ring holding them together: a short chain ending in a bullet with a hollow shell. Its copper red had become yellow on account of being handled so much. It was the very one that he had carried with him constantly since the first days after we charged the provincial government building in Tikrit. It had appeared when the name Qashmars first appeared. It was the same bullet that remained in my father's hand, the one he hadn't inserted into the anus of the young man harassing Istabraq, the youth whom the market's beasts of burden had saved that day. I don't know how my father had hidden it during the torture sessions and kept the very same one with him over the years. And then, how had he brought a bullet here through the airports?

There were posters of nature scenes on the rest of the walls. The accompanying text indicated that they were German landscapes. There were other large posters of half-naked women in seductive poses, feigning ecstasy. The lips, as usual, were in that form I had started to hate for its vulgar repetition: the half-open and slack-jawed mouth forming a circle, pretending to be ready for a kiss. I don't know who it was that put into the minds of women that this primitive pose was seductive. I had started casting my first glance at women's lips whenever I would see them in newspaper photos, advertisements, and calendars. As soon as I saw them adopting this commercialized expression, I sensed their extremely naïve phoniness, and all sense of attraction would evaporate. I would turn the page as a way of refusing to include myself in the herd of consumers who fell for that sort of thing.

My father's snoring got louder.

On the opposite side of the room stood a wooden entertainment center. A television was in the middle, and the rest of its shelves were crowded with books, videotapes, cassette tapes, and several vases made of clay and glass, together with dozens of identical glasses. There was another familiar motif that appeared in many houses, namely, the family photos that stood in the corners of the shelves. In this case, of course, it was my father with Rosa in various places and different cities. Of these, I recognized the Barcelona seashore and Baghdad, in front of the Freedom Monument. The photos were leaning on their stands atop the books, which were all lined up together, spines facing out, with the exception of the Qur'an. It stood on the top shelf, leaning against a multivolume Qur'anic commentary, its cover facing out, decorated with the word "noble" written in gold.

I continued looking around in this way for about half an hour, during which I got up and walked around with still constrained steps. I checked out the inside of the kitchen and the bathroom, looked over some of the book and movie titles, and took one look from the window into the courtyard and another from the middle of the living room into the room where my father was snoring. The rhythm was variable and some of the snores startled me, as though he were about to choke.

During this time, I got my breathing under control, my pulse returned to its normal rate, and I became more comfortable with the place. So all that remained was for me to begin the encounter with my father. I approached him softly and put my hand gently on his shoulder. His snoring stopped. I paused, too, before repeating a call that I hadn't practiced for many long years. I was like someone whose voice was catching on the words, like someone feeling them out and recalling their rhythm, drawn from the secret, unknown places of the spirit. In such a situation, a person feels the words like a physical touch that makes the choking tears flow:

"Dad. Dad. Dad!"

He twitched, rolling onto his back and mumbling heavily, "Eh? What?" He opened his eyes with difficulty, and then the surprise widened them. "Oh! Saleem!"

He sat up right away, rubbing his eyes like a lazy child and trying to hide the effect of the surprise upon him by saying,

"Good morning! What time is it?" Then he got out of bed and added, "It must be Fatima who sent you." He followed that up while looking for each of his shoes beside the bed by saying, "She's a good kid, a respectable girl."

We went out to the living room. His hair was messed up, and traces of gray could be seen at the roots of the dyed locks. He looked around for something: he was looking for cigarettes. He shook the pack that was near the television, opened it, then crushed it with his fist and threw it on the floor: "Damn! Empty."

"I have some cigarettes," I said.

"What kind are they?"

I took my pack out of my pocket and showed them to him. He said, "No, these are lights. They don't do anything for me. Have you eaten breakfast?"

He had turned toward the refrigerator, opened it, and stuck his head inside, saying, "We need milk." He followed that up with a joke: "But the cows are out to pasture!"

He laughed and gave my shoulder a pat that hinted at our connection. I felt then that he was closer to the father I had known in the past. It was as though the phrase about cows, spoken as a clear allusion, was a sign of all that we had shared in our distant village.

I said, "I'll go down and get some milk and cigarettes. Which kind do you want?"

He pointed to the crumpled pack on the floor. "Those. Or just tell the Chinese people in the store across from the club—do you know it?—tell them, 'I want cigarettes, milk, and German cheese for Mr. Noah.' They'll know what you want. In the meantime, I'll get the coffee ready and take a shower. Okay? Here, take some money."

"No. There's no need. It's not much at all." I took a chance with his amiability and added, "And I cordially invite you to breakfast in your own house."

We laughed with an affection that brought us closer. I went out with a trace of a smile on my face that lasted until I reached the entrance of the Chinese store. It was true: as soon as I let the Chinese shopkeeper know what Mr. Noah wanted, she brought it to me immediately. I returned, carrying everything back up to the kitchen while my father sang German songs in the shower. I smiled and began preparing breakfast, arranging it on the coffee table after clearing off the pile of newspapers and ashtrays, leaving his bunch of keys, connected to the bullet, in its place on the edge.

My father came out of the bathroom, revealing his enormous stature and his predominantly gray chest hair. He had wrapped a wide, white towel around his waist. When he saw that the table was ready, he said, "Eat, if you want. I'll be right there."

"No, I've already had breakfast. This is for you. I'll just have a cup of coffee with you."

He went into his bedroom and came out after a few minutes in different clothes, clean and elegant. He had combed his hair and tied it back in a ponytail. He gave off a piercing scent of perfume. I knew he liked to go overboard with perfume, to the point of literally pouring it on his body. It was an old habit that he hadn't given up. He was following the model of Grandfather, who had constantly repeated, "Prophet Muhammad loved three things in this world: perfume, women, and prayer."

My father ate with a voracious appetite while I hesitated, uncertain as to how to begin the conversation with him. So it happened that he posed most of the questions at first. As he chewed each mouthful, he asked me about myself: my health, my life, my work. He said he hadn't known that I was here in Spain, and that nobody from the village had known anything about me. But personally, deep down, he had felt confident that I was fine and in some safe place. He used to reassure Mother whenever she would cry because she missed me, and he would invent stories about how easy life was for those who had emigrated from Iraq. He endeavored to comfort her, while she continued beseeching God on my behalf during her prayers.

At that point, I started asking my questions about Mother. He said, "She is just as she was: a great woman who bottles up her sorrow and keeps on slaving away. Now she takes joy in raising her grandchildren. Istabraq lives with her in our house. Istabraq got married to your cousin Ibrahim. She wanted to name her first son Sirat, but Ibrahim refused. He was right to do so, for reasons you well know!"

We laughed, and I learned for the first time that my father knew the story of Istabraq's love for Sirat.

He continued, "And so she resorted to the Qur'an for a name, like all the rest of our family. Her health has gotten much better. She now has three children, and I left her pregnant with a fourth. She has become much fatter, and she is not that skinny 'Reed' that you knew her as. By the way, she hung a large picture of you in the front of her room, and every day she lifts her children up to it, saying, 'This is your Uncle Saleem. He is going to return, bringing you lots of gifts.' The result is that they spoke your name before they spoke the name of their father."

My father finished eating his breakfast. He reclined next to me against the backrest of the couch and began to smoke with pleasure. He seemed to be more focused, livelier, and more prepared to talk. So I followed his lead and started smoking and asking questions, even frank ones.

I asked about nearly everything apart from the two essential questions that I didn't dare broach: Was he the one who killed Grandfather at dawn that day? Or had he exploded in Grandfather's face, just as I had seen before leaving, after making sure that Grandfather had already died? Secondly, where did this passion for women come from? For that matter, how did he make love to Rosa, who loved him and was so intensely jealous of him, given that they had ruined his manhood and his testicles in that electric torture session?

So I circled around these two questions like a butterfly hovering around a flame, taking care not to be burned. Among other detailed questions, I touched on the village, the family, and how things were going there. He answered me at length and sometimes with his own commentary.

We talked together and smoked for more than three hours, during which my father would get up and move around the room waving his arms whenever he was affected by the force of what he was narrating. He would sometimes clench his fists and grind cigarette butts between his teeth, looking like someone acting out a tense scene in a play.

I know I'm incapable of recording here everything that was said, and of describing his movements and his pauses in detail, given that my surprise at his words completely overpowered me. So I'll summarize the main events he told me, beginning with the day in which I journeyed from the village, the same day in which Grandfather journeyed from this world.

"Everything changed, Saleem. It changed utterly."

CHAPTER 11

T he village buried its sons' bodies. Then it submitted to the orders of the government, whose institutions applied the pressure necessary to rapidly transform it into a normal village like all other Iraqi villages.

"There was some satisfaction in burying Grandfather at the highest point of the cemetery. They put green banners above his tomb, as well as jars of salt for visitors seeking a blessing to lick. The sick would cut strips from the banners at his grave to tie around their necks or forearms, like consecrated amulets. The people were satisfied as to Grandfather's heavenly reward, he who was considered a blessed man and one of God's pious saints.

"Relations with Subh were restored in the traditional way. Its people stopped winking to each other at our surname` of Qashmar, not out of respect for us but out of fear of the government, which had imposed the name Faris on our village, and which possessed eyes and ears that spied into every corner: on both banks of the river, on both sides of the mountain, on the dry land and the water, in the air and in the mud.

"An atmosphere of war pervaded the entire country. The television, the schools, the party organizations, and the police were all instruments of the government for mobilizing and exercising control. There was iron and fire. There was fear and repression. We gave ourselves over to waiting and to a faint hope in an obscure salvation. It felt like our hope hung by a thread."

"The people gradually disengaged from Mullah Mutlaq's domination after his passing. They were brought into submission by the government's vicious authority. The sessions for religious studies in the mosque were dissolved, as well as the meetings to solve social problems, which were transferred to the city courtrooms. The number of people who prayed got smaller, and no one talked any more about avenging our honor, which they had pledged to the mullah. I didn't do anything about that. But inside, I held fast to my covenant, which I had pledged by my soul and sworn in front of my father. It was only I who kept living under the authority of the venerable Mutlaq, eagerly maintaining my obedience to that authority, no matter what the cost.

"As far as I was concerned, Saleem, my father was everything to me, everything: the absolute authority in this life and the next. You, yourself, saw my relationship with him, how sacred he was to me. He was history, religion, values, the absolute, and the single existing truth, or else the source of these things. In my eyes, he was the strong, knowledgeable, and completely correct man. Disobeying him was out of the question. He raised me that way from the moment I became conscious. Engraved into my emotions and my makeup was the dictum that 'God's satisfaction comes from the satisfaction of parents,' so his contentment was my greatest goal. Actually, in my eyes, my father was God's sole deputy on earth. And I confess now, to you alone and for the first time in my life, that I would often see the Lord incarnated in him. He represented direct divinity for me, according to what his upbringing established in me. I never once, in all the days of my life, dared to look into his eyes.

"One thing alone interfered with that assurance of mine regarding his divinity; one thing broke it. And that was regret. Yes, for regret is a human characteristic, and a god cannot regret anything he does since he is omniscient in his knowledge, his perception, his control, and his desire. When I say regret, I mean that your grandfather, my father . . . . My mother informed me one day at noon during a harvest season long ago that the only thing my father had done and regretted—something he had regretted having done throughout his entire life, even to the point that it sometimes made him cry in her lap in moments of weakness—was having cut off part of his first wife's finger when she had pointed it menacingly in his face. Everyone knew about the incident and used it as an example, but what no one knew—apart from my mother and me, and now you—was that my father regretted it, and that references to this incident continued to torment him. Meanwhile, it helped me by stripping him of that quality of divinity.

"On account of this too, I was eager to act in a different way toward you, my children. I had doubts, or rather, I was certain about my inability to enforce a strict upbringing like my father. At the same time, I was wary of imposing upon you an image of the divine father, as happened to me. So I was impartial, human, and friendly, as you have observed.

"I would practice with you my other half, my living, normal, human 'I.' Internally, though, I was and still am divided in two, Saleem. One half was content, obedient, and convinced of the holiness that my father represented, as well as committed to working now for the sake of the hereafter. The other half was suspicious, rebellious, doubtful, human, and committed to the world. It loved laughter, women, wealth, poetry, rebellion, and sin. I would practice the first in the village, in the presence of my father, and the other there in Kirkuk, at work, with foreigners, or with the Germans, to be more precise. But with you, I was eager to be neutral and to avoid letting my fierce inner struggle affect you.

"Your grandfather was a great man, Saleem. But he may have been born in the wrong era. I loved him greatly, but I wish that I had found a way to be free of his control other than by being loyal to him in every detail. At the same time, there is another half of me, which you have no doubt noticed here and consider improper. I have let go of its reins, and I don't make excuses for it, Saleem. I have set it free from its prison that lasted so long, allowing it complete freedom and liberty until it vomits up every repression. Or until I see where it takes me.

"But don't ever think that my first half has died, or that it has abandoned its controlling and censuring role. Instead, I'm like someone who is on a vacation or taking a break after having long practiced a certain way of life, and who will resume that way of life one day. Indeed, I find that it is the first half who sometimes continues to dominate. It is he who uses the other half for his own purposes like this. It is he who pushed me toward the fateful adventure that carried me here. He rides that bridled other half and paves the way for him, all for the sake of fulfilling his obligation, his covenant, his oath of vengeance before your august grandfather.

"I don't know if I've expressed this entangled nature in my soul very well, or if I have satisfied you with my answers and this explanation of mine. Or if I have disappointed your hopes. I don't know if I have been a good father to you or the one you wanted.

Because my father, who kept me from pleasing myself, was the same one who kept me from thinking about pleasing others.

"Well, I'll try now to sketch things out for you as they actually happened by telling you the story which brought me here. Or rather, the story of my arrival to this place.

"After your grandfather's departure," (he didn't say his "death" or his "murder") "I was in a state of the most intense conflict with myself. Your mother was the only one who realized this pain. But she continued to be just as you knew her: a magnificent woman who acted as a mother to everyone. I used to go to my father's grave and cry over him there. I would recite the Qur'an for him to reassure him that I still had it all memorized, just as he had wanted. I would whisper to him, speaking with him, asking him questions, and feeling that he was answering me. I would confirm the covenant that I had made with him and my commitment to everything he wanted from me, especially my oath of vengeance. And would you believe that I didn't dare look at his headstone, either? Instead, I would rub it with my hand and then kiss my palm. And when I would leave I would hear his voice calling me: 'Listen, Noah!' He would repeat his famous saying, and the mountain would echo it back: 'If a dog barks at you, don't bark at it; but if it bites you, bite it back! . . . bite it back! . . . it back! . . . it back! . . . back! . . . back!'

"I was away from my job in Kirkuk for more than two months. When I went, intending to offer my resignation, I learned that they had fired me for being gone so long and had appointed someone else. They gave me the rest of the money that I had earned along with a good severance payment.

"Then I went to my Kurdish friend, Kaka Azad, a man of great wealth and even greater sorrow. My relationship with him had become very strong during my years of working there, given that I used to go to his restaurant to store my belongings and confide my secrets. He would often take me to his house, where he lived alone. We would stay up late, and I would spend the night there. In the morning, he would drop me off at work in his car.

"Azad has a long and bitter story too. To make a long story short, the government had killed his family and destroyed his village. He found it utterly demolished when he returned from one of the trips that he used to take to Iran and Turkey, smuggling both goods and people. So he too swore to take revenge. He doctored his identity card and settled in Kirkuk after opening a magnificent restaurant there. He used it to find out what was going on and get close to men in power, whom he would lead on gradually until they poured out information to him about themselves and what they knew. Azad would pass this information on to the rebels in the mountains. He would also use it to plan his own schemes.

"I used to talk with Azad about everything, and our friendship deepened to the point of brotherhood. With an oath on the Qur'an, we pledged our brotherhood to each other one dawn at the prayer niche in a mosque, and we each gave our new brother a hair from our mustaches. I don't deny that in doing so I was still imitating my father in that he took a Kurd as his brother. Do you remember? Sheikh Abd al-Shafi, the one we visited for Istabraq's treatment.

"My brother Azad taught me much. If your grandfather nourished my blood with the essential meaning of values such as dignity, manliness, and good morals, Azad poured them into my bones like cement and taught me how to practice them with a firm heart. He taught me the rigidity of stubbornness. He would dedicate each operation he undertook to the soul of one member of his family, and when he had reached the last one, he would start over, in the same order, dedicating further operations to them. I also learned from him how to wear masks, to practice contradictory roles, and to perfectly embody different personalities to the degree that I confused myself with them.

"When I informed him of my covenant with my father, and of my oath to insert this bullet" (he took his keychain and shook the bullet in his fist) "into the anus of that fucker who was the cause of everything, Azad patted me on the shoulder and said, 'I envy you because you know the face of your enemy. Your job is easy. You aren't like me. I'm fighting an enormous, faceless octopus of an enemy: the men in power, in the party, in the army, and their supporters. Rest assured, you will fulfill your vow. You will also avenge your son who was killed in their war, together with the other sons of your village, one by one.' I wished that my father could have heard us then. I wept, and we embraced.

"Afterward, we decided to relocate to Baghdad. He sold his establishment in Kirkuk, and together we opened a splendid restaurant between Saadun Street and Abu Nuwas Street. At the time, I told your mother that I was journeying to fulfill my oath, and we shared the following exchange. I said to her, 'I have been pleased with you.' She said to me, 'And I, with you.' She knew what an oath on the Qur'an meant. And she knew very well what my father had meant to me, he who had signified the same value and preeminence for her. I told her that I didn't know how long I would be gone. I didn't know where I would settle or where I would go. I didn't know, while I was away, whether I would live with or marry other women, or whether I would die. If she wanted me to divorce her, I

139

would do it. Otherwise, let her forgive me for what I might do, or what I would be forced to do, or what would happen to me.

"She cried, of course, and said, 'Do whatever you want. I don't want a divorce from you. Your being my husband and the father of my children is an honor for me. You are my crowning glory, and I want you to be my husband in the afterlife too.' She remained strong in her convictions and came to understand me. She even gave me strength and resolve by encouraging me and promising that she would take my place in managing the house and the family. She would beseech God on my behalf in her prayers. In exchange, she asked me to spare no effort in searching for you. I promised her, and then we bid each other farewell. She offered me her gold jewelry, but I told her that I had plenty of money, some of which I gave to her.

"Then I departed, like you, one dawn long ago, and I haven't since gotten in touch with her. What's more, I haven't even been concerned with my promise to ask about and search for you. That couldn't really interest me.

"In Baghdad, our restaurant became a favorite among important officials, people of influence, and the rich. We would seduce them with our hospitality and our flattery. We acquired their friendship and facilitated their depravity. In this way, we learned much about them. At the same time, we inflicted upon them many carefully planned attacks. We gathered critical information, which Azad delivered to the rebels and the opposition. We learned that the young man I was searching for had been appointed as some kind of attaché in the Iraqi embassy in Spain. That's how we began looking for some way to get me to him.

"Then it happened that some officials from the Ministry of Information came with a delegation of Spanish tourists to our restaurant for dinner. I met Rosa, and one thing led to another. Wait a second, Saleem! Don't think that I used Rosa and deceived her, even though, to be honest, I wouldn't have hesitated to do that. I've done much worse in the company of my brother Azad. But what happened to me was the coming together of my goal and my emotions, for I actually loved her, and she loved me. She is the only woman that I have loved and chosen by myself, for myself. As you know, your grandfather chose your mother for me, and the first time I met her was on our wedding night. My love for your mother is strong, but it isn't the typical love between a woman and a man. How can I explain it to you? I mean, we were a very successful couple, but we weren't passionate lovers. As for Rosa, I fell in love with her and chose her purely out of my own desire. There were many things that brought us together. And so it came about that she undertook all the arrangements for my coming here. She spoke with the Spanish embassy and the immigration office, she signed the documents and the required guarantees, and she paid the fees for everything, including the flight here.

"We settled first in Barcelona; then I persuaded her to come to Madrid and set up this business with me. But she doesn't know anything about my other objective, which I've made good progress toward achieving. I've compiled plenty of details about when this animal comes and goes, about his house and his favorite places. And I've acquired the trust of two strong thugs who will help me, professionals from a Colombian gang. They're ready to make a move any time I want. Executing my goal and fulfilling my oath is nearly accomplished. The only question is choosing the appropriate time and place. So, what do you think?"

CHAPTER 12

certainly didn't think anything at that moment. I just reeled from the sudden shock. My father, who clearly noticed my surprise, didn't insist upon hearing my immediate impression, nor did he object when I changed the subject. I invited him to come out with me and pretended to focus my thoughts on resolving Rosa's fury.

He said, "You go ahead to the club and wait for me there while I call her now. We'll see what happens."

I found the club's outside door half-open. I stuck my head in and called to Fatima, whose voice came back to me: "Come on in!"

I slipped in without opening the door any further. As soon as I got down and looked around, I was taken by a second surprise of an altogether different kind, which lessened the bitterness of the earlier one with my father. The place was as clean and neat as if a team of professionals had just then installed the furnishings. In fact, Fatima had just succeeded in getting everything in order. She was putting on the finishing touches and spraying air freshener, circling around and aiming it into the corners.

She smiled and asked, "So, what do you think?"

I was able to give her, of course, my immediate opinion: "Amazing! How did you do all that? You're my hero!"

Her smile broke into a contented laugh. She went behind the bar while asking me if I wanted something. "No," I said. "I'm waiting for my father to come down."

"How was he when you saw him?"

"Fine," I said, but I was quick to change the direction of our conversation to anything else. I asked her, "How's your hand doing?"

"Perfect. I told you it's just a scratch. If only all our injuries were like this one!"

Then I turned to routine questions along the lines of whether she would be going home or whether she would work today. This was interrupted after a little by the sound of the door being thrown open. My father came in, vivacious and happy, spreading his arms like a stage performer and boisterously calling out: "Ta da! Fatumi! Fafy! Good morning, my dear!"

"Hi, Mr. Noah! Good morning! How are you doing?"

"I'm as strong as an ox, as you can see! Saleem and I are going to have lunch. Do you want to come with us?"

"No, thanks! I have to go home. I need some more sleep, and we have a lot of work ahead of us tonight too."

"Listen, if you don't want to come, you don't have to. Just give me a call so that I can arrange something. I do especially need you to be here tonight, but you worked so hard last night and today that you deserve more of a rest."

"Don't worry, Mr. Noah. I'll be here for sure."

"Fine. In that case, to pay you back, I'm also giving you Wednesday off, in addition to your usual Monday and Tuesday."

143

My father patted my shoulder, saying, "All right then, let's go, Saleem! You go now too, Fatima. We'll see you tonight. And you can arrive late, if you want. That is, after midnight, when the party gets going. See you later!"

We went out, and he led me to the Chinese store to buy another pack of cigarettes. His mood was convivial there too, and he joked with the woman behind the counter. He kept repeating a few words in Chinese, which I understood to be a greeting, and a couple other words that may have been obscene because the woman laughed and replied, turning them back on him, "No, no! You are, you are!"

After that, we left, and he led me from one narrow street to another and through several alleyways until we arrived at a traditional Spanish restaurant, whose façade testified to its antiquity. The scent of ancient wood wafted out as soon as we went inside. My father had been calm on the way there, admiring the pleasant weather, praising Fatima and the goodness of the Chinese shopkeepers with banalities that were nothing more than attempts to fill the silence. He tossed a few coins near the head of a vagrant sleeping in one of the corners, saying, "Poor guy, he's got AIDS."

Nevertheless, I noticed how he resumed his exuberant manner as soon as we entered the restaurant, calling out to the waiter there and addressing him by name—"José!"—who, together with another friend, responded with a similar affability and intimacy. My father directed me toward a seat at a table in the farthest corner of the dining room, next to the window that overlooked the alley. Meanwhile, he stood with the men at the counter and explained our lunch order, jumbling the pronunciation and the sequence of the Spanish words and resorting to gestures at the menu or samples of the dishes on display.

There, in the corner illuminated by sunlight coming through the window—the clock facing us pointed to nearly four o'clock in the afternoon—we partook of our food, drink, cigarettes, and conversation slowly and deliberately.

We went back to fill in the details of what we had covered in our earlier discussion and to finish up numerous episodes. He expressed his overpowering desire to call Azad to let him know that he had found me, saying, "This would make him very happy."

He followed that by saying, "But I can't do that because we agreed that I would only call him when I had carried out my goal. At that time, I will call him without making any indication, implicitly or explicitly, about what I have done. Just the call by itself will mean that I have completed the task. We will simply exchange greetings, ask how things are going, and talk about other, normal things. Do you know, we also agreed to make the pilgrimage to Mecca together, as soon as we are free from the tyrant's regime. Then, we will repent before God, be purified for our sins, and pursue righteousness.

"I tried to convince my brother Azad more than once that he should marry and start a new family. He's in a position to do that from the standpoint of health and finances. But he continued to refuse, saying that he had taken an oath upon his soul to marry and bear children only after the tyrant falls. He doesn't want to bring other children into the world who will be subjugated by the dictator or the mere sight of his face."

Then I told my father what I had heard and read in the news about the intention of the United States to assemble a coalition and attack Iraq if it didn't allow inspections and the removal of weapons of mass destruction.

He exclaimed, "What weapons of mass destruction? What is there that's more destructive than the dictator himself, who kills and drives out millions? Why don't they just take him out and save us?"

We argued about politics after that. I rejected an attack on Iraq under any pretext, and he said that salvation from the dictator was something for which we ought to pay the highest price. I told him, quite deliberately, that Germany, for example, refused to participate in an alliance like this.

His answer surprised me: "Of course. The Germans are a great people, civilized and respectful of the laws. And a filthy affair like a dictator needs an opponent to match, such as the American president. The Americans put the dictator there, and they ought to take him away. Afterward, we'll know how to take care of them, for it is easier to fight the thief who is a stranger than the thief from inside your own house."

The political discussion not only revealed to me another side of my father, but it was also a view of the bitter state of affairs there in Iraq, where the long-suffering hope for a release from oppression was now exhausted. Up to this point, the conversation had revealed to me how much my father held on to his other personality, to vengeance, and to the demands of religious obligation. Now I sought to call forth the other side of him so that I could see both sides together at the same time, or at least, so that I would be able to sense the power of each, relative to the other.

I asked him whether he had spoken to Rosa on the phone, and how she had responded. The enthusiasm in his voice fell a little, and he lit another cigarette. He said she was very angry with him and that he hadn't been able to understand anything except her refusal. He couldn't hear everything she said because she was sobbing violently on the phone as she cursed him.

Then he commented, savoring the carefully enunciated words, "She seems like a wounded bull, to use a Spanish expression. Or like a wounded lioness, to use an Iraqi one. She's like that. I understand her. And I don't hold it against her."

There was silence for a few moments, and he began to stare out the window. I asked him what he was thinking of doing. He sighed and shifted in his seat, putting his hands on the table and shifting his gaze to scrutinize my face in a serious and direct way. He said, "I don't want to take you away from your private life and drag you into my affairs. But I need you. I need your help. Can you do it?"

I had been slouching on my side of the table, but now I sat up straight in my seat, alert and curious.

He went on, "Rosa is very angry with me. And she's right to be angry. I understand. But I'm also certain of her love for me, and a passionate woman is always ready to forgive. Indeed, she wants to forgive and looks forward to it. But at the same time, she's waiting for some creative or special apology. That's the price she feels will earn her forgiveness. Gifts, flowers, and special words are appropriate, of course, but with every new falling-out, it's necessary to search for a new and fitting apology.

"Therefore, I was thinking that you could go to her. Yes, you! Tomorrow you could go to her house in Barcelona. I could give you her address, her telephone number, the location of the flower shop and the type of flowers to buy, the words to say, and the appropriate time. That way, it would all be a big surprise for her. She knows how important my children are to me, and you in particular. This would also be a way for me to acknowledge my love for her in front of my family, which is important to every woman. A woman feels more confident whenever she sees her lover introducing her and acknowledging her in front of people she knows are important to him. This arrangement would also be a good opportunity for the two of you to get to know each other better."

(At that moment, I thought again about asking him what his relations with women were like after what had happened to him when he was tortured, but I didn't dare.)

My father demonstrated his characteristic tone and fluency in putting forth his wisdom, as well as with his persuasive style. To a certain extent, this presentation surprised me, and to the same degree, I liked how intelligent it was. A certain feeling of satisfaction came over me because he was restoring our close relationship in a significant way. Or maybe because I felt that he needed me. So I wasn't refusing, and indeed, the matter intrigued me. But I told him I had to work, and that it wouldn't be easy to go to Barcelona, solve the problem, and return, all in the same day, then go to work immediately. For that reason, we had to think of some way to arrange a suitable schedule for it, or he needed to give me time to ask for a few days off.

And here came my father's final surprise, which he expressed with more certainty and desire than the previous two. He said, "What do you think about leaving your job and coming to work with us in the club? We—no, I need you to be there. We'd pay you a better salary, and you'd be free to choose your hours. You would be one of the managers, not one of the regular employees."

I smiled, and I may have gasped like someone who had been splashed in the face with cold water. I responded, again not refusing, but with an answer like my previous one, saying, "But I don't understand the least thing about your work. I don't have any experience in it at all!"

He leaned back, knocking the ashes of his cigarette off to one side while shaking his other hand to make light of the matter: "No! These are minor issues. You don't need experience or professional training for this work. You could take charge of the cash register, for example, or of ordering things we need and negotiating their prices and transport. You know, general administrative issues. Really, Fatima can teach you all the other aspects of the job in one night. These are minor issues, Saleem, minor. So, what do you think?"

CHAPTER 13

When he heard my assent, I saw his eyes flash with a restrained desire to jump up and shout for joy. He reached for his wallet and said, "Take a plane to Barcelona. It's faster and more comfortable."

But I'm one of those people who prefer traveling by train. It makes me feel as though I possess the freedom for long reflection, which flows easily with the rhythm of the train's motion as it darts through various landscapes. How pleasant it is to sit near the window, looking out at the movement of the ground and the trees, rivers, hills, villages, cities, animals, mountains, plains, fields, and clouds. A long parade of open land and spacious skies. During such times, my mind wanders freely: reviewing, remembering, analyzing, planning, dreaming. Unbroken silence and undisturbed reflection, alternating between the internal and the external. If I'm not contemplating the view, I'm pondering my inner life, and vice versa. While my eyes are focused on one, the mind's eye excavates the other. Or one of them will bring me to the other by invisible channels of insight. Moreover, train travel has a romantic character, impressed on my mind, perhaps, from watching old movies filled with encounters, farewells, lovers waiting at train stations, or wandering journeys (like mine, now) for the sake of remembering and reflecting. The director usually chooses seats by the window for those characters too.

So it was that I didn't read more than seven pages of the book I brought with me. I became distracted in recalling the previous night, my first night of work at Club Qashmars, where my father danced with a joy that I knew perfectly well was the result of my being there with him. My agreeing to what he wanted had a big part in it too. After performing his comic opening monologue, he undertook Rosa's role of general oversight without neglecting his own role of circulating among the customers. Even though he always had a glass in his hand, he didn't finish more than two beers throughout the night. He had also arranged that things wouldn't go on as late as dawn, as happened on other weekends. By some clever adjustments, he managed to bring the night to an end by 3:00 a.m. Perhaps he was thinking about Fatima's fatigue and my own after my first shift, and of my journey the following day. But he definitely didn't notice Fatima's and my delight at our growing intimacy and physical contact.

I kept recalling last night's feeling that barriers between Fatima and me were collapsing. She was teaching me how to manage the accounts and take the customers' orders. She also pointed out to me the different kinds of drinks and how to prepare and serve them. She was doing double duty, performing her own job and training me at the same time, and we were together behind the bar throughout the night's enjoyable work. She moved like a bee, buzzing between neighboring flowers, never forgetting anything and always flashing her smile. During that time, due to the narrowness of the place, one of us would often bump into or brush past the other. We felt this contact to the core, and we would shiver—a delicious shudder—even as we feigned indifference and apologized routinely to each other at first. But after it kept on happening, we began to be content with a smile, even when we did it on purpose sometimes.

During all those collisions, I wasn't able to stop my arms from repeatedly brushing against one of her breasts. Nor could I avoid rubbing my thigh against her butt when I passed behind her in order to take something from one of the waitresses in the lounge while Fatima was bent over to take out more appetizers and olive cans tucked away on the floor under the lowest shelves. My thigh brushing past her butt. It's an image I'd replayed many times since last night, and now again very deliberately, like a movie scene in slow motion, frame by frame, as though immersing myself in a detailed examination. To be honest, I was just taking delight in it all. My thigh, as it rubbed against her right buttock, found it soft, firm, round, and succulent all at once, like a child's balloon inflated by his mother. Then my thigh continued its advance, descending into the depression between her two buttocks like a train passing down through the valley between two hills. It sent a shiver passing from my thigh to my loins. My thigh continued its intimate caress onward and up the other buttock, feeling that it had spread them apart a little. I trembled as I imagined it.

The work wasn't as hard as I had imagined it would be. On the contrary, I found that I liked it, especially in that it allowed constant interaction and working directly with other people, something that I had lacked and consequently suffered from in my former job. I was just a driver there, and my relationships were limited to my friends at work such as Antonio, Mario, and Mario's girlfriend, Carmen, as well as the owner of the distribution agency. For that reason, isolation and loneliness were the defining characteristics of my life.

This work was entirely different because it provided interaction with different kinds of people. Indeed, it forced you to find strategies to communicate with them and understand them since the idea was to win them over as customers. It was something that had other advantages too, such as the shifts passing by quickly and being full of energy and life, never boring. You don't feel any fatigue or boredom at the time, but afterward, when it's over and you decide to take a rest, you're exhausted, and your legs hurt from having stood for so long. But you do get to rest.

I wouldn't say that what I felt for Fatima was an irresistible or unavoidable love. Instead, I might be able to describe it as the common situation where you follow the lead of the head, not the heart. There is another person who you believe suits you, the sort you want to be in a loving relationship with. You realize perfectly that you will truly come to love her. Then you start living together. After you get to know her better, you start to feel that she is right for the kind of relationship that might end up with your becoming partners in life, a married couple. So it's not something that started with an irresistible first glance, nor with obscure feelings of attraction and seduction that overpower your self-control. Rather, it was a kind of persuasion and choice. Or even a kind of conscious and planned intentionality.

As far as I was concerned, this is what I felt toward Fatima. At least, this is what I thought, which is more correct than to say "feel." The experience was entirely different from my bewildering passion for Aliya, who was my first love, and perhaps my one and only. To me, her small eyes were bewitching and impossible to resist, for in them I saw life's pleasure and meaning. It's true that Fatima had large eyes and long, black eyelashes of the sort that I know general, traditional taste considers to be fascinating. Without a doubt, they were enchanting eyes. But they didn't do to me what Aliya's eyes did.

As for Fatima, it was possible for me to communicate with her, and there was both affection and sexual attraction. She was a good person, suitable to me, and ready to enter into a loving relationship. I could love her. Her glances, her way of interacting with me, the tone of her voice when she talked to me, her reactions, her affection, and her constant smile all confirmed that she felt the same contentment and willingness that I did. Indeed, taken all together, it formed a kind of call that invites you to the next, familiar step.

There is a certain kind of feeling, which no doubt everyone has experienced or heard about. It is the feeling that the other person across from you shares the same satisfaction and the same readiness. There is an aspect of silent, mutual understanding, and the other person is waiting for the right moment to begin building the relationship.

The additional thought came to me that my father was aware of the matter, given things he had suggested or joked about with one of us while the other was nearby. Deep down, he may even have been wanting it and planning for this relationship to happen.

For the whole seven hours to Barcelona, the lion's share of my reflection went to Fatima and to remembering details from the previous night. Far fewer were my memories of Aliya, which wove through my other thoughts and would usually overpower me whenever the train passed near water: a river, a lake, the sea.

Meanwhile, there was a single thought that I expelled from my thoughts as often as it pushed itself to the front of the line. That was my father's decision to fulfill his oath. That oath had brought him here with a goal, namely, to insert the remaining bullet from that youth's revolver into the anus of this diplomat in the Iraqi embassy; that is, the very same anus.

I felt a severe difficulty in swallowing this thought. It seemed so incomprehensible to me, at least after the marks that ten years of experience in the West had left upon me. I could only see it as a kind of recklessness and an inhuman cruelty, a sick behavior leading to disastrous results. How could I divert my father from it, when it was his goal and the vow he swore on the holy book in front of Grandfather?

I wasn't able to think clearly about the matter, and I didn't see an obvious method for dealing with my father since this issue was so central to his life, his thought, and his determination. So I turned my mind back to remembering some of the specific recommendations that my father had given for this mission of mine with Rosa. He had spoken a lot, but I was content to focus on the essentials, which were that I buy her a bouquet of large, white jasmine flowers from a shop close to her house. I was to bring them to her after attaching the card that he had written on and folded up. I had used the interlude of his writing the card to read a book, not feeling any curiosity to see what he was composing. Nor had I cared much about memorizing the details of what he wanted me to say to her. I would let the meeting and the conversation proceed spontaneously since all that he wanted was that she be convinced and come back to him. Therefore, if she wanted that deep down, there was no need for much talk, and likewise if she had decided in her heart to leave him.

So I decided to be content just to say things with the purpose of getting her to come back. That idea would be my guide for the natural direction of our conversation. The only thing I had to do was bring her a jasmine bouquet and ring the doorbell of her house at the address which he had written for me. I wasn't nervous, nor did I feel any uncertainty about how to interact with her. Indeed, I had a strange confidence, or something like that. It was as though we knew each other well. Perhaps that feeling came from how well I understood the Spanish personality and culture in general. Or maybe a certain coldness and nonchalance on my part, if I can put it like that. Many who know me describe me that way. I sometimes think that it's due somehow to Aliya's effects upon me.

In any case, I knew where I was going in Barcelona perfectly since I'd spent two weeks there during last year's summer vacation. It had drawn me in with its mixture of ethnicities as well as buildings. The extremely old and the extremely modern lived side by side, regardless of when they were established. And the festive atmosphere of Las Ramblas Boulevard, which was always a delight to walk up and down, day and night—I'd go between one end leading to the sea and the other leading to the crowds in the vital city center.

What I liked most about Barcelona were the two things that in my opinion are the legs upon which this city's surprising and attractive personality stands. These are the sea and the imprints of its genius, Gaudí. I spent days there, never bored, drawn in by what could be described as an expansiveness, an enormity, a richness, or a universality that leads you with a jolt or a soothing playfulness to touch both sides of the existential anxiety. Something gives you the sense of interacting with nature in its vastness. Indeed, as a whole, the city seems to form a majestic cosmos in and of itself, and not just be part of one.

Barcelona also has a spirituality, inspiring its visitors with the extent of its varied, uninterrupted history. It takes you in and recognizes you as family in some way, by the strength of its life, its greatness, its sweetness, and its festivity. I wonder what my father likes in Barcelona.

I arrived at four in the afternoon. My only luggage was the shoulder bag that I usually carry, in which I had packed some books to read, a notebook and paper, pens, Kleenex, a pack of cigarettes, and a small comb. That made me the first one off the train. I headed straight for the train station's bathrooms, where I emptied my bowels, my bladder, and my nose. I washed my hands and face with cold water, and I put water on my hair, running my hands back and down to my neck. Then I took my little comb out of the pocket of my bag and fixed the hair on my head, my eyebrows, and my mustache. I left the bathroom feeling alert and refreshed.

I took a taxi in the direction of Rosa's address. But once there, I didn't ring the doorbell at the front of her building. Instead I headed directly to the flower shop, which I found just as my father had described it. I bought a bouquet of jasmine flowers and slid the card out from between the pages of my book. I asked the young shopkeeper to tie it to the jasmine bouquet, which she did with an elegant, colorful thread.

After that, I went to the café next door, where I called Rosa. She was shocked by the surprise and said she would come immediately. I selected a table for us by the window, near a small glass fountain. The surface of the water was distorted by light from multicolored lamps submerged at the bottom. I ordered a café con leche, which I sipped as I smoked and stared through the window at the door to Rosa's apartment building.

Rosa came out. She was wearing a white dress with a collar decorated by pink ribbons. On her arm she carried a purse that resembled a basket because it was made of dried plant leaves — perhaps hemp or palm fronds?

Rosa was tall and voluptuous, with blond hair that flashed in the light of the late-afternoon sun. She swung it from side to side as she watched for traffic and hurried straight across the street, without going to the pedestrian crosswalk. She came closer, moving quickly, her ample breasts bouncing under a white bodice and two necklaces. One necklace had silver beads and the other's were a yellowish white, bone colored or else actually made of bone. Whoever saw her would never suspect she was nearly fifty. And here is her perfume coming through the door before her. She greeted the café workers. It was clear they had known each other for a long time. Then she looked around for me. I lifted my arm to wave to her, and she rushed over. We embraced.

She sat down across from me, unable to contain her joy, which she emphasized by repeating, "What a surprise! My goodness, what a lovely surprise!"

The waiter come over and asked, "The usual?"

She nodded to him and continued telling me how happy she was. I hastened to push the bouquet of flowers over to her, which I had put on the seat next to me. They made her gush, "Ooh la la, how beautiful! Thank you so much, Saleem!"

"Don't thank me," I said to her, "Thank the one who sent them. He wrote the card."

Her fingers tore open the envelope and then the card, which had more than one fold. When she lifted the cover, it began to play softly the music of "Happy Birthday to You."

"Oh! Because tomorrow is my birthday!" Rosa sighed deeply, and as she read her smile radiated passionate love and rapture. She didn't notice the waiter, who put a full glass of beer, very tall in the German style, in front of her and then withdrew in silence.

Meanwhile, I lit another cigarette and sipped my coffee, watching her face intently. I saw tears stream from her eyes. She let them drip onto her lips, which contorted with emotion and radiated joy by turns. At that moment, it would be impossible for anyone looking at her to doubt, even a little, the depths of this woman's passion for Noah.

She closed the card and pressed it to her breast. Then she kissed it and burst into tears again. I hurried to pass her a Kleenex I had taken from my bag. She wiped her tears and laughed with a mouth tightened by emotion, saying, "Your father is crazy. And I'm just as crazy because I am madly in love with him."

At that moment, I regretted not having read what he had written to her in the card. I don't know exactly how it happened, but I got up and went around to the other side of the table and hugged her where she sat. She cried on my neck for a while, shaking and a little hysterical. I let her squeeze me to her for a while until she calmed down. Then I kissed her forehead, helped her wipe away the tears, and went back to my place.

"Thank you, Saleem," she said.

She had calmed down and took a sip from her glass. She smelled the bouquet of jasmine flowers and set it next to her on top of her purse. Then the words burst out: "I've never loved a man the way I love your father! When I found him, neither my heart nor my soul erected any barrier to keep him from coming in. I felt that he was the very man I had always been waiting for. Precisely him.

"There were many things we had in common, such as our love for Germans!" (She laughed as she said it.) "Did you know that ever since I was a child, people at home and at school called me 'the German Girl'? It's because I look so much like them. This blond hair of mine that you see, this is its true color; it's not dyed. And my body frame with its wide shoulders . . . . As far as I was concerned, the whole idea appealed to me from early on. For that reason, I studied German as a second language, something which I continued at the Goethe Institute. Ever since I was young, I've traveled nearly every year to Germany.

"My first conversation with your father in his restaurant in Baghdad began with this topic too, and right away I felt . . . . It was as though we had known each other for a long time, for his first words to me were 'Are you German?' I answered him in German, saying, 'No, I'm actually Spanish, but they say that one of my grandmothers was of German descent.' He immediately sat down next to me, and we began speaking in German. He kept insisting, half-serious and half-joking, that I was a German hiding in the skin of a Spaniard. We talked about the differences between the two peoples and cultures, then about Goethe, whom we both loved. He astonished me when he began reciting long passages from his poems by memory.

"The difference between German women and me is that I'm a chatterbox. Just the opposite of them, I love to talk a lot." She laughed and commented, "I'm a perfect Spaniard in this regard, and this is the only thing that your father doesn't like in me."

I nodded, remembering my father's complaints about this very thing when we had lunch the day before. He had said, "The only problem is that she's a chatterbox. Listen to me, brother! She gives me a headache talking nonsense until very late at night." He had gone on sardonically, "Sometimes I think that the dictator is kinder to my head than the torture of her chatter.

At least the dictator repeats the same pompous, worthless expressions, so your ears can block them out and get some rest. But this woman, in the café and the street, at home and even in bed lying on the same pillow, pours her nonsense directly into my ear canals!" He had smiled and added, "But all the same, she is a good person, she's honest, and she's generous."

Rosa continued to prattle, narrating her life and dwelling on every stage. Her father had been a famous gold merchant in Barcelona. She was her parents' only child. Her husband, an Argentinian, had also been a gold merchant. She had separated from him without giving birth to any children, and she put the blame for that on him: "I didn't love him. He was an excellent businessman who was able to continue running the family business after my father died. But he was too practical, and I'm a romantic."

Rosa pointed through the window at the façade of her building and said, "I own this apartment building as well as a shop in the city center, which I rent out for a good price. Three years ago, I also bought a small, pretty house in the suburbs of Berlin. Whenever I can't cope here, I flee there for a month or two. If I am German in shape and culture, your father resembles them in his stubbornness!" She laughed. "We say here that the stubborn man has a square head. Just think, he is crazy about Germany like me, but every time I tell him that we should go live there, he refuses, saying, 'Not now. Later. Later.'"

I listened to her more closely at this point, trying to figure out whether she was aware of his true motive for insisting on staying in Spain, and specifically in Madrid, namely, the secret of the bullet keychain. When I noticed that she was moving on to talk about something else, I asked her, "And you don't know the reason?"

"No," she said. "He merely replied, 'Not now. Later. Later.' He's just stubborn. Didn't I tell you that he has a square head?

But look, his heart is round. He hides in that body of his a heart that is enormously good, kind, and sweet."

"Do I gather from all this that you accept my mediation and will come back to him?"

She laughed. "Of course! Certainly! I'd go crazy or die if we ever parted. I will take the plane this very night. Can I reserve a seat for you to fly with me?"

"No, I'm too tired. I'll spend the night here and come back tomorrow on the train. I love trains."

"In that case, I'll give you the key to my apartment. As for me, I can't wait until tomorrow."

She went on talking, and I heard her without really grasping what she said. I was content simply to nod my head while thinking of an appropriate way to ask her about how the two of them made love, given what I knew of my father being ruined during those distant days of electric torture in Tikrit. Finally, I decided to try.

"I have a question that I'm hesitant to ask, but I'm very curious to know the answer."

"Ask, Saleem, ask! You are dear to my heart, and we're friends, aren't we?"

"Yes, certainly! But it is personal and private. You don't have to answer if you don't want to."

She reached out her hand and patted mine. "Saleem, Saleem. There are no barriers between us now. And you ought to have the confidence to trust me with your secrets, if you want to. Didn't I just tell you all about myself without holding back?"

"Yes . . . yes. It's just that I was wondering . . . I mean . . . for example . . . I find it strange that you are as extremely jealous about him as you are, and—"

She interrupted me with a start, "How could I not be jealous of him? He's my lover. And he, the naughty bastard, knows how to treat women well. In some incomprehensible way, he has the ability to charm most women. I know him well, and I know his tongue. You, no doubt, know him too."

I didn't want to tell her that I actually hadn't known that about him at all and had only noticed it recently, here. When I had discovered it, I was both astonished and perplexed: the images of him collided in my mind. What she said didn't give me my answer, but the conversation encouraged me to keep trying. So I continued with a certain reluctance that was both real and feigned, "No, I mean . . . . But promise me that my father won't find out what I'm asking you about."

She lifted the gold cross on her necklace to her mouth and kissed it, saying, "I swear to you, Saleem. I'll take your secret to the grave with me. You can trust me."

"I mean . . . what I'm trying to say is . . . as a man and woman, as any man and woman, you and him . . . you know . . . I mean, in bed . . . . "

She laughed, reclining her broad shoulders against the seat back. Then she leaned forward and said in all seriousness, "Ohhh! I see what you mean now. I see what you mean. Listen, your father has amazing fingers. He knows how to play the entire instrument of the body with a skill that puts the best musicians to shame. My God! I have never experienced the pleasure and delight that I enjoy with him with any other man. He has strange and surprising styles, such as using dates— don't ask me how! And his tongue too. Oh, what a tongue he has! And what knees! And . . . .

"As you must know, a woman, and especially a romantic woman like myself, isn't looking merely for meaty appendages in a man. Rather, many other things draw her to him. Love is not just the short moments in bed, but rather the coming together

163

of many little things. Such as the masculine traits in his behavior, his mindset, his personality, his way of speaking, the tone of his voice, the nature of his glances, the way he touches me, as well as where and the timing of it. The feeling, when I'm next to him, of confidence, strength, and affection. And . . . ."

She went on speaking about love, lovingly.

CHAPTER 14

There are people who are happiest when living in a constant state of activity. That's why they talk about many projects, even if these projects will never see the light of day. They fill their closely scheduled time by lining up promises, appointments, and engagements that are only words. Some of these people appear very busy when actually they are not, for at the very least, making you think they are pressed for time gives them a feeling of importance.

On the other hand, there are people, such as myself, who prefer the details of their lives to be clear and defined, easy to control and arrange. Therefore, any unsettled matter makes them feel that they, too, are unsettled, and creates a kind of anxiety that keeps them up at night. Maybe my habit of isolating myself after every important conversation or event comes from this. I run through each episode and analyze it as though I'm trying to fit it into what I believe to be the order of my life. Perhaps this too provides an explanation for my flight from Qashmars Village when the corpses were rotting, when I felt suffocated because I had no way of putting that difficult situation back into order.

I put forward this introduction in order to discuss the most important matter that was still unresolved and kept me from sleeping. That was my father's goal of ramming the last bullet into the anus of the diplomat who was a reckless youth once upon a time. My father's smiles and his intimating winks, which I always interpreted as a sign of the secret between us, confused me. I was frightened by the thought that a moment would come when he would disclose the matter to me and ask me to join him. I would certainly refuse, but the problem, which I couldn't resolve, lay in how I might turn him away from carrying out this deed. Especially since I knew that it was the fundamental goal behind this strange journey of his. It was for this ultimate purpose that he planned, acted, worked, behaved politely, and suffered. It was the oath in front of Grandfather, and he'd never feel at peace until he fulfilled it.

Here I was after having spent approximately one month working at the club. I found myself fitting in and satisfied. Indeed, I was thrilled with this kind of work, perhaps because of its energy, the sense of renewal that came from always seeing new people, and the convivial atmosphere. There was also the feeling that I was free to be present, late, or absent, given that I was a manager and not just a low-level employee.

The final factor was that my relationship with Fatima was progressing toward its expected outcome. We officially became a couple after we declared to each other what was in our hearts, our minds, and our desires. The physical contact on a daily basis at work led us to further contact out in the street, in the presence of our close friends, and at home. She repeated her request, when she was kept late at work, to spend the night at my place, until in the end I provided her with her own set of keys. The marks of a woman's presence in my life and in my house became obvious. We opened ourselves up to each other completely. We touched and kissed, we slept together in my bed, and we decided together what clothes to wear and what movies to go to on our days off each week. She informed her sister, whom I was soon helping with some of her homework. I told my father and Rosa, who said they knew and gave us their blessing. In the same way, our regular customers learned about the matter, as well as our friends, my Cuban neighbor, and the building doorman.

I was perfectly aware that Fatima wasn't Aliya, and that my comparing them was not appropriate because I didn't want to force her to adopt behaviors that were not part of her true personality. Every individual has their own separate being, something I'm always aware of deep down. But I wasn't completely able to pull up Aliya's roots from my spirit. Consequently, I wasn't entirely able to avoid drawing comparisons between them. Fatima had wide eyes, with attractive, black pupils—striking in the midst of the surrounding white. Aliya had small eyes that burned my spirit. Fatima had thick, African lips—double the size of Aliya's delicate ones—which made a fertile soil for plucking passionate kisses.

The lovely thing about it all is that, from time to time, I was able to persuade Fatima to smear our fingers and lips with dates and date nectar. We would suck at each other gently, drowning in each other's kisses. She found the idea strange at first, but she got used to it. Indeed, she began to relish the pleasure of it, which gave me a sense of comfort, satisfaction, and victory. It was as though I began to see in this matter something that was essential to who I was, especially after Rosa alluded to the way my father used dates. I had been surprised at that, but her comments allowed me to understand better why there were dates in their Madrid apartment, as well as an abundance of them in her Barcelona house where I spent the night alone.

Their apartment had been very neat, as though intended for tourists. When I saw the plants and the flower vases filling its walls, I remembered that my house lacked plants entirely. How did that happen when I was from a family of farmers, while Rosa is the daughter of a gold merchant? At the time, I didn't reflect on the matter for long, contenting myself with the first justification I found, that everyone seeks what they lack. But I thought that, in the future, I would put something green in my prosaic home. Instead of focusing on that, I was occupied during the train ride back by thoughts about my father's fingers and the dates, which led me to wonder about Grandfather's insistence on a well-stocked bag of dates in our house. Was Grandfather like us too?

The thought came to me that the three of us resembled each other in many ways. Perhaps we were actually one person multiplied across bodies and generations. But we were different from each other in many things too. Was it humanity's way of attempting to attain perfection? And what was this special character in our relationship that makes each of us secretly desire to educate, or re-educate, the other? I wonder, do our similarities outweigh our differences? Were we truly three people, entirely independent of each other in our existence? During that journey, I boarded the train with many questions: though it carried me until I reached my destination, I didn't arrive at any answers.

One night, when I made a move to have sex with Fatima, she apologized and said she didn't want to, that she preferred to wait for marriage. That made me very happy because it was what I had actually been hoping for and wanting myself deep down. Perhaps it was a kind of resistance till the end against succumbing to sin, given that Grandfather had planted in my conscience a fiery fear of the punishments for iniquity. I told her I agreed, indeed, agreed happily, and that I had been very reluctant and had only intended to have sex because I thought that she might doubt my manhood. I also thought that her living in the West for several years would have influenced her attitude toward something like this. She revealed to me that she had done it only with her former husband, and that for her part, she was firmly committed to resisting any fall into sin. So we did everything together with the exception of intercourse.

Another factor that brought her closer to my inner world was that she reminded me of the appointed times for prayer. Moreover, she resumed her own practice of praying, intermittently at first, then regularly.

I certainly spoke to Fatima about Aliya a lot, and her eyes teared up when she saw me crying as I described the scene of Aliya's drowning. She embraced me very tenderly, allowing me to pour out all the tears I had in me. Afterward, she didn't show any jealousy over Aliya's place in my memory. And she laughed when I told her about the poems that I used to write for Aliya and Aliya's reaction to them.

As our discussion of poetry broadened, Fatima learned from my responses that I still wrote poetry, and I learned what she thought about it. She was entirely indifferent toward poetry. Rather, to tell the truth, she actually didn't care for it, even though she claimed, like everyone else, that she liked it. She recited from memory some lines of classical poetry that she had memorized in her school days. But she hadn't memorized or read anything beyond this. At the same time, she had memorized the words to heaps of Arabic and Spanish songs. She asked me if I would show her some of my poetry. I tried to refuse in order to avoid any possible discord, but in the end I agreed, thinking it necessary for her to know about what interested me.

"I don't know where I put what I used to call poems. Wait a moment; I'll look for them. They might be folded into the pages of one of the books that I was reading four years ago. Under my bed there is a box containing some of them." The dust rose up, and I sneezed. "Here's one. Should I read it to you? No, I'm too embarrassed to do it. No! Well, okay, I'll read it as an example. Listen. Of course, the person meant here is Aliya. Listen:

> More precious than light in the dark prison cell
> Sweeter than dates to the man who is fasting
> Her lips, two dates
> Her fingers, rare fruits
> Her eyes . . . speech fails
> Shyly she passed, piercing the clouds with her glance
> A peasant girl she bloomed, overlooked by the politicians
> Her nipples are forbidden to the passion of men
> Yet permitted to the water and the breeze on the roof
> She will decamp to the unseen, and you will spy her
> Never, ever again.

Fatima smiled at my mention of the dates, and when I finished, she clapped gaily and said, "I like it!" Then she asked innocently, "Is it poetry?"

It came to me that she didn't even know about the existence of modern, unrhymed poetry. I dove into an exposition of modern verse, citing folk songs and the poetry of al-Sayyab as examples. So in the matter of poetry, she differed from Aliya.

I had a deeply rooted conviction that Fatima was the right woman to share the rest of my life with. It was even more clear that she would be my wife. We happily discussed our relationship in this way and made plans to find an appropriate moment to bring the subject up with our families. Was my father, too, trying to find an appropriate moment to let me know that he had decided on the time when he would carry out his mission? This single thing was what most disturbed me and made me anxious. For here I was, finding my life to be in order. As far as I could tell, all its details were organized and clearly understood, especially in regard to work, women, and the future, which I could now almost see.

It almost happened that I broached the subject myself. I would transform my anxious waiting into a matter that was in my own hands. But it was hard for me to find the right way to start. And what ideas could I put forward? How could I form an argument strong enough to turn him away from what he had resolved to do? So it was, as often happens in life, that the moment came on its own, without any decision on my part or his.

It was during his first visit to my apartment. He came a little before noon for some work-related business. He also said he wanted to see the home to which I had invited him more than once. The first thing that startled him—as happens with nearly all visitors to my house—was the overwhelming sight of pictures of Iraq covering the living room's ceiling and walls. What surprised me was the difference between his reaction and everyone else's. After he had wandered around more than once, staring at them and approaching some to examine them more closely and identify the scenes, he gave me a long look, biting his tongue on several responses. It was as though he were cycling through them to find the one that expressed what he wanted. And that was the case, for after he slapped one hand against the other, he stood in front of me, crossed his arms over his chest, and said, "What is this, Saleem?"

His censuring tone provoked the echo in my question. "What do you mean?" I blurted out.

He said, "I used to think you had better sense than this. That you didn't give in to the sick nostalgia that afflicts most exiles, who imagine that everything is beautiful in their abandoned countries, even the ruins and the garbage dumps."

"But it's our homeland, Dad," I protested. "My homeland."

He uncrossed his arms to illustrate his point, shaking one of them in the air. "No! True homeland is that which we fashion for ourselves, just as we want. Not as someone else makes it, like the tyrant did. That's not the kind of homeland we want. That's why we abandoned it. Homeland is like love. It is a choice, not an obligation. If you must put up pictures of a homeland, then put up the ones that you, yourself, want, or even those that you have made on your own. No, no . . . ."

He was shaking his hand toward the pictures as though saying goodbye to them or refusing something that the walls were offering him. He turned around in a circle where he was, and then he sat on the couch, heaving a deep sigh. He continued to express his disappointment, "No, no. I used to think you had better sense."

His words provoked me. I felt as though he were tearing down my kingdom, which I had built and arranged with persistent patience over the course of years. In my loneliness, I had invented a complete story for nearly all these pictures, a history, a world. His arrogant dismissal—in a single moment and so easily—of everything that I had established and lived with happily throughout my ten years of exile here enraged me. I felt

172

as though he had killed my entire family with a single bomb, a family I had formed out of long effort, love, and private dreams.

Therefore, as had just happened to him, I fell silent, searching for the decisive response that would avenge my soul's wound. I exhaled deeply in my turn and found that I was shaking. My body temperature was rising. I quickly sat in front of him, looking into his eyes with a stormy challenge and a feeling of strength that I had never before known in myself. As a result, my words came out choked and agitated, strikingly aggressive: "And I used to think you had better sense too."

My words surprised him, of course, and he asked, "How so?"

I picked my chair up and set it down further back, moving away from him a little. I said, "That you would do all this for the sake of achieving a backward, foolish, and insane goal like shoving a bullet up someone's ass. You are deceiving Mother and abandoning your family. You are deceiving Rosa and exploiting her. Then there's this radical betrayal of your entire personal, moral, and religious heritage. All that for the sake of a foolish goal!"

I felt both power and relief after saying that, especially when I noticed that I was able to anger and provoke him as much as he had me, if not more. His face contorted and flushed as though I had stabbed him. He wiped his face with his palms and shook his head back and forth as he attempted to absorb the blow and regain control of his emotions. When he spoke, there was a change in his tone of voice that testified clearly to the difficulty he had maintaining his composure.

"I haven't deceived anyone. Not your mother: I was up front with her about the entire thing, just as I've already told you. And not Rosa, whom I actually love. I also haven't betrayed my moral and religious heritage, as you say. Indeed, the complete opposite! What I'm intending to do is a serious and sincere

173

fulfillment of that heritage. The only reason I'm breaking my back here is to fulfill an oath I swore on the Qur'an in front of a person who is gone forever. If I were not fully committed to my moral heritage, there wouldn't be anything else forcing me to fulfill an oath like this."

I spoke in a still-belligerent tone: "What kind of backwardness is this? And what madness? We are now in a different era, a different country, a different culture! No one will understand an act like this. What you are intending to do will even be considered a serious crime, and the law will condemn you for it."

Worked up, he rose from his seat, displaying his customary behavior when he's angry. I would describe it as theatrical, not because he was acting, but because of his intensity. He paced around the room and gestured with his entire body. Every moveable part of him was shaking to the rhythm of words that seemed to be ripped forcibly from his bowels.

"Where is this era of yours? And its culture and laws, while it sees us massacred on a daily basis in our country, right before its eyes? Hell, even with their support sometimes! Huh? Where? Where?"

He was truly frightening as he circled around me like a raging bull, right around my chair, which made me stand up in front of him as though by instinct. Meanwhile, he kept on yelling and kicking the wall. I was certain that if we had been in his house, he would have started smashing everything in his path.

"Well? Where are the laws and the civilization of this pathetic, hypocritical, despicable, fucked-up world? It sees us driven like innocent sheep to the slaughter. Well? Yes, say it! Say clearly that you don't want to help me. You can be sure that I'm not asking you to. I don't need you for it. I wasn't counting on you. You were right to let me know where you stand before I made myself believe in you any longer. Well, say it then! Speak up! You're afraid, cowardly, a pussy. You're chicken shit, a traitor. You're all fucked up!"

That's when I somehow brought my face right in front of his. We were standing like roosters in the fighting pit, all puffed up. I shouted, "I am not a coward! The truly cowardly thing is what you intend to do. So you are the cowa—."

He slapped me on the face with his entire strength, knocking me to the ground. Then he left, slamming the door with a violence that made the whole building shake.

CHAPTER 15

When Fatima came that evening, she found me completely naked, submerged in the bathtub. After my father had slapped me and slammed the door behind him, I remained lying on the floor for a while, sobbing. His palm had paralyzed my face. I reached out to the lowest of the pictures and pulled it down. I began to rip the pictures off the wall and tear them up, bitterly running on at the mouth, "I don't want a homeland. May God damn it and everything else! I've only known pain there, and I've only carried pain away with me. My homeland is Spain. No, not even Spain. I don't want any homeland! I don't need a homeland."

I stared at the shredded pictures in front of me. Then I started sobbing with a dejected tenderness, "But Iraq . . . Iraq! Dad!"

I got up onto my knees and tried to put the torn pictures back in their places. My insides surged with tumultuous, conflicting emotions. An inner rage brought me to my feet in a madness, and I began tearing down the hanging pictures and scattering them like chaff. I felt my right cheek with my hand: the stinging had started to burn even more. I staggered into the bedroom and ripped up everything there. Then I threw myself on the bed and wrapped myself up completely in the blanket. I rolled myself as tightly as I could into a fetal position, as though embracing myself. I cried there and shook, like a child who has received an entirely unexpected punishment from parents who had been caressing him. My delirium came in waves that crashed over me in the darkness under the covers. I was tossed back and forth between cursing everything and repeating my father's phrase: "This world is all fucked up. This world is all fucked up."

I decided I would never see my father after that day, that I would cut him off and remove him from my life completely. It would be as though he had never existed—he, my family, Grandfather. "Ah, Grandfather! How much I need now the extreme tenderness of your fingers caressing us in the sick bed! I am now in my bed, Grandfather, alone and hurting. But you might side with my father because he wants to carry out your every wish. Or else just because he is my father, and you would always say that it's not permitted to criticize one's parents or talk back to them for 'he whose parents are displeased will not obtain God's favor.'

"I'm sorry, Father. I've sinned against you. I was insolent toward you and raised my voice inappropriately. I deserved more than a single slap from you for that. Forgive me, Father. But I'm not comfortable with what you want to do. I tried to divert you because I love you and I'm afraid for you. Yes, I'm afraid. Not because I'm a coward, as you believe, since this fear of mine is of another sort. Do you understand? Do you understand me?

"Throughout my exile I would see you sit me down, a child, on your knee, with your feet in the shallows of the Tigris, as you read Goethe's poems to me. Why can't you be the person whose back I longed to clasp when riding our donkey on the way to the highway? Tender moments, during which I would feel that my small heart was embracing your heart through my ribs and yours. As far as I was concerned, even the odor of your armpits was the most fragrant thing I ever smelled. We would wave to each other, and I would keep watching as you got further away. I would wave and wave until the car would disappear with you, a black dot on the black line of the road. Your slap today—was it a wave in our final parting?"

In the darkness under the blanket, internal billows shook me. I felt as though my sweat formed waves that met the surge of my violent tears and the flood of pain rising up behind my face. I don't know how long I remained like this. Then I got up, heading toward the bathroom. My right cheek was less red than I had expected, given that I imagined it would be stained with blood. I washed my cheek with cold water and said, "I need water. Water, Aliya, water."

I filled the bathtub, throwing all my clothes on the floor. I stretched out in the water and leaned my head against the edge, sinking in up to my neck, to my ears. I needed to not hear anything. I needed to not hear myself, or my father's slapping me, or his slamming my apartment door. I sank to my ears, to my chin, until I was suffocating . . . until Fatima came and fell upon me with a broken heart: "Saleem, baby! What's wrong? What happened?"

She squatted next to the tub and took my head, pressing it to her chest. Like my mother, like Aliya, like Grandfather in his moments of tenderness. Maybe I cried again. Fatima raised me up compassionately and wrapped me gently in a bathrobe, embracing me. It was like when my mother would snatch me out of the washing basin, crooning songs of the harvest, tea, and rain:

Rain, rain, O high rain
Lengthen the hair of my head
My head, head, O my high head
Rain on the people.

She would take me joyfully and smell me, as though I were a ripe apple. Then she would kiss me and say, "My God, how sweet is my little Saleem. My baby is clean! My baby is clean!"

Fatima said, "Come to bed, baby." She stretched me out under the covers for a second time. She arranged the damp hair of my forehead for me, brushing it away from my eyes with fingers like feathers. She kissed me on the forehead and on my nose, and I brought her fingers to the surface of my right cheek, where perhaps the stinging had subsided, where perhaps the red had disappeared. Maybe that was the case since she didn't ask me about it. Or else she saw it and imagined it was from leaning against the edge of the bathtub. She didn't ask me about it and was content to repeat her question, "What happened?"

And I repeated, "It's nothing, nothing."

After a while, she continued, "I found the club closed, and when I rang at your father's place, Rosa came out to me and led me away from the door, whispering that something had happened between you two—I mean, between you and your father, Mr. Noah. She said he was lying in bed, drinking, smoking, and shaking. That he was in bad shape. She just told me something had happened between you two, nothing more, and that we wouldn't open the club for work today. And she said, 'Go, Fatima; stay with Saleem.' What happened, Saleem? And why are all the pictures torn like that? You're shaking."

"Nothing. It's nothing. Or, yes, I sinned against my father. I raised my voice against him and behaved shamefully. Do you know, Fatima, that my father never once looked into Grandfather's face? Never! He respected him and revered him as one ought to. But me, me . . . !"

"Take it easy, baby. Everything will work out. It's okay. Everything will turn out fine."

"No! I'll never turn out fine!"

"Rest now. Rest, and I'll make you some green tea."

I didn't leave the house for two days. Fatima took care of me as though I were sick. She helped me carry out my desire of taking down all the photos, and she gathered the ones I had shredded into a single box. Sometimes she would caress my lips with her fingers and joke with me, openly flirtatious, "Do you want dates?" The longest that she was gone was to go bring me a pack of cigarettes, to shop, or to visit her sister. I later learned that she would meet with Rosa since she wouldn't speak with her on the telephone except to exchange a few words, mostly just repeating, "Yes . . . yes . . . okay."

Then Rosa came to me on Friday morning. Fatima had left me on the pretext that her sister needed her that day and that she had to take care of a few household chores like washing clothes, sweeping the floors, and shopping. She said that she would come back in the evening, "and your food is ready in the refrigerator."

Rosa embraced me and wept as she interceded, "I'm begging you, Saleem! Come with me to visit your father. He's killing himself like this. He doesn't eat. He only drinks alcohol and smokes. He sometimes sleeps, shivering and delusional in his bed. He hits his head with his fists; he punches, kicks, and head-butts the walls; he knocks his head against the iron of the bed. He's destroying everything. He's destroying himself! He's in agony, Saleem. I accepted your mediation between us—do you remember? So accept my mediation between the two of you. I'm begging you. He'll kill himself if he keeps going on in this way. He's torturing himself because he slapped you, and he isn't telling me the truth about what happened. He just slaps himself all the time and says, 'I struck Saleem, Rosa! I'm an animal. I'm an animal.' Please, Saleem, come with me. Because he'll kill himself like this. And if something awful happens to him, I'll die too. Please!"

I went with her, taking along two packs of cigarettes and a heart beating with noisy commotion. She opened the door for me cautiously and whispered, "You go in; I'll stay here."

I saw my father lying on the couch in the dark living room. His hair was disheveled. One arm was hanging off the edge of the couch, holding a glass, and he took a drag from the cigarette in his other hand. As soon as he saw me, he rushed over to embrace me. We cried on each other's necks, each of us asking the other's forgiveness. He said he was a failure of a father, and I said I was a disrespectful son. "Forgive me! Please forgive me!"

When we stepped back from our embrace, I found him turning his right cheek to me, saying, "Hit me! Hit me!"

"No, Dad! No!" I kissed his cheek and embraced him again.

He seemed thinner to me, exhausted, defeated. I had never seen weakness like this in him before. When we had calmed down, we sat down next to each other on the couch with empty glasses all around and an overflowing ashtray on the coffee table in front of us. We felt more united than at any other time. We felt our loneliness and our true exile in this "fucked-up" world more than ever before.

Now that calm had the upper hand, I wondered whether I should take advantage of the situation by making it a condition of my forgiveness that he abandon his determination to carry out his goal. But I contented myself with leaving things as they were, for I was the one who needed pardon from him. Moreover, I wanted to avoid stirring up the subject a second time.

But during our subsequent conversation, I found myself indicating what I wanted in another, less forceful way, with feigned neutrality. He was the one who brought the subject up when he exposed the truth of his hidden weakness, or more precisely, what I knew to be his strength. He revealed to me the struggle inside himself over this issue, for he was, as he put it, caught between two fires. One of them was what I earlier called his moral and religious heritage. I knew the power of an oath on the Qur'an, especially because he had given it in Grandfather's venerable presence. I also knew the meaning of vengeance and its importance, to the point of holiness, in our social customs.

The other fire was his private conviction, which suited both his personality and my own, that he, in all honesty, rejected violence and the culture of revenge, and that he disapproved of fanaticism. "Believe me, Saleem, even if I appear in the hide of a wolf, I have the heart of a meek lamb." He said that if he carried out his goal, he would regret it and torture himself. And if he did not carry it out, he would regret it and torture himself then too.

"You will not regret it, Father, and you will not torture yourself. Believe me!"

"But I took an oath on the Qur'an, Saleem. I made a covenant with my father."

"It says in the Qur'an, 'God will not blame you for speaking rashly in your vow.'"

"I wasn't being rash. I was speaking honestly and seriously in my oath."

"It was the effect of the moment. It took place during an exceptional moment, filled with anger and devoid of clear thinking. God is great; he knows this and everything else.

Grandfather will understand when things are clearer and more open in the world to come."

I supported my argument with what I remembered from the Qur'an and the sayings of the Prophet, especially when I noticed how easy it was for my father to accept them. It may have been that he, at his core, wanted a justification from this exact source. "The Qur'an also says, *If you dole out punishment, dole it out according to what was inflicted upon you. But if you exercise patience, verily, that is better for the patient ones.*"

"And Azad? What will I say to my brother Azad?"

"Tell him anything. That you carried out the deed. Or that the person you were pursuing wasn't the right one. Or that he went off to another country, in an unknown direction, to hell. Or that he died. Or anything! Or tell him the truth about your new conviction. Indeed, you could even try to persuade him to stop the series of his acts of vengeance and reprisal. The principle of an eye for an eye is bitter, Dad. It's true that we're the ones who established it, but humanity's subsequent experiences have shown that applying it will, in the end, leave us all blind."

"It's not that simple, Saleem. I've piled my hatred upon this person for all these years. How could it be possible for me to rid myself of all that in a moment?"

I was silent for a little while, conscious of how the speech had poured from my tongue and how easily the wisdom had come—if it is permissible for me to describe it in this way or to ascribe such a thing to myself.

"In order to get it all off your chest, I think it would be good to call him right now on the telephone. Make him hear everything you want to say."

I got up and took hold of the telephone book, flipping through its yellow pages, while he looked on with a grave expression. The cigarette was never far from his mouth, and a cloud of smoke wrapped around his face. Then I heard him say, "I have his name and telephone number."

He pulled out of his pocket a small address book and opened it up. He held it out to me, pointing to the name and number.

Without looking at his face, I began to turn the dial of the telephone, and when a woman's voice answered, I asked her to connect me with the person in question. "Please, it's important."

She said, "Just a moment, please."

I held the receiver out to my father and began to watch him. His hand was trembling, his lips quivering. After some short moments of waiting, he burst out in a loud, choked voice, "Why?" Then the awful shout poured out of him to the point of shaking his whole body, "Why?! Why have you done all this to us, you criminals?! You ignoble pigs! You bastards! You—"

Through the phone's receiver, I heard the other line being cut off, then the dial tone came on. Meanwhile, my father continued shouting, "Why? Why?"

I fell upon him with a hug as he broke into tears, gasping like a slaughtered bull. Rosa burst in anxiously. She embraced us both together, asking desperately, "What happened? What happened?" Then she hurried to the kitchen, coming back with a jar of water, which she used to wash my father's face and give him something to drink.

After some time—I can't say how long exactly—of this burning rage, the likes of which I'd never known in my life, and which I doubt I will ever witness again, my father calmed down more than we expected. He was like someone who had vomited out the poisonous food that was hurting him, as though the "why?" was a hurt that had been eating his heart. Little by little, the pallor in his face subsided.

At that point I said to him, "What do you think about us going together to the mosque today for Friday prayers?"

I read a sort of relief in his features, and he nodded to me in agreement.

"In that case, I'll go home now while you shower and eat something. I'll come to get you."

I kissed him and went out. Rosa's glance followed me, filled with gratitude and questions. She still had one arm hooked around my father's neck and was holding a jar of water in her other hand.

CHAPTER 16

After we left the mosque following last Friday's prayers, my father shook my hand. "May your prayers be acceptable in God's sight!" he said, giving the customary blessing. "Thank you, Saleem." After he was quiet for a while, he added, "I didn't expect to find so many Muslims here, or this beautiful mosque."

He was calm, as though his heart were made of still water. A halo of spiritual contentment clearly enveloped him. I felt at the time that I had regained my father, finding him much as I remembered him to be. So I decided to stop digging up whatever he was hiding. I would stop wondering about it entirely. I would forget. Or, to be more precise, I'd pretend to have forgotten it all, especially everything connected to how Grandfather died. And I wouldn't ask if he had given up his goal of fulfilling his oath, or whether he had only delayed it and would carry it out without my knowing.

I reinforced this resolve with what the mosque's preacher said, even if I was only using it as an excuse: "O my brothers, God says in the Qur'an, *Don't ask about things that, if they become clear, will hurt you.* It is not necessary to know everything. If sometimes there is a comfort in knowledge, at other times ignorance and forgetting have a comfort that is even greater."

I felt a certain satisfaction as I recalled my sense in recent days that the details of my life were coming back under control. I painted the walls of my living room, covering the nail holes with white. My father dyed his hair black. Fatima said that her family had agreed to her marrying me.

"All that's left is for us to inform your father!"

My father and Rosa, after having confirmed that everything was ready for the party that night, were sitting harmoniously in front of us on the other side of the bar, looking very elegant. My father said to me with a laugh, "Your hair has gotten long. Do you want me to cut it for you again?"

My father hadn't stopped drinking and smoking, but more than once he had mentioned his intention to cut back. I remembered how he had said to me a couple of days earlier, "I think that it would be good for us to try to go to the mosque every Friday." He raised the glass that was in his hand and added with a smile, "At the very least, in order to cut back on our sins!"

It was evening, and just the four of us were in the club. The two Spanish waitresses hadn't arrived yet. My father and Rosa were whispering together happily. Fatima murmured to me, "Come on, let's tell them."

"Dad, Rosa. Fatima and I have something we'd like to tell you."

"We have a surprise for you too."

"What is it?"

"No, you two go first."

"Fatima and I have decided to get married."

187

They leapt up together out of their seats, joyfully congratulating us and reaching across the bar to grab our heads and kiss us. Then they said to pour us all something to drink, and we began clinking our glasses and exchanging celebratory toasts. "We'll put on a huge party for you here!"

In the midst of the jubilant commotion, Rosa asked, as any woman might, "And what will you name your children? I mean, for instance, if the newborn baby is a girl?" This may have been her way of creating a greater sense of familial intimacy and letting us know the extent of her hopes. Or maybe she said it because she found in us a way to experience vicariously her unrealized dream of being a mother.

Giving me a significant glance, Fatima responded, "I know what it is."

My father said, "And I know too."

"What?" Fatima asked him.

My father looked at me and said, "Aliya."

Fatima jumped up, clapping for him, "That's it! That's it!"

We clinked our glasses again, joining their music with our laughter. After a pause, Rosa said, "And if the child is a boy, I would suggest that you name him Noah." Her hand massaged the back of my father's head.

But he interjected with a tone that was meant to be ironic, "No; that's a bad omen. What sin has the poor little one committed to deserve our making him carry my misfortunes?" His smile widened, and he stared at me, sure that his irony would strike home this time when he said, "We'll name him Sirat."

We gave each other a high five like kids, bursting out in loud laughter to the surprise of the two women. I was carried away by the energy of the laughter to take it further, commenting, "But will we add the dot to make it Dirat?"

We gave each other another high five, and my father fell back from the force of his laughter. When he regained his composure and sat back up, I said in all seriousness, "We'll name him Mutlaq."

My father clasped my hand and said, "Yes, that's good."

Then Fatima asked, "And now, what's your surprise?"

Rosa looked at my father, saying, "Should I tell them or you?" Then, without waiting for his response, she went on, "We've decided to move to Germany and leave the club and our apartment to you, if you want them." Smiling, she added, "Provided you pay the rent, of course!"

My father said, "We are also going there to look for friends from my oil days in Kirkuk: Kristof and his wife, Sabine."

The Spanish waitresses came in at their usual time, a little before darkness fell, and of course, the reasons for our festive atmosphere were revealed to them, which led to abundant kisses all around. This delight that some people show in sharing the happiness of others, or a person's empathizing with the concerns of another, always touches an emotional cord in my breast. It sometimes moves me to tears, as happens to me when watching this sort of thing in the movies. I know that this sympathy of feeling is intuitive and as ancient as the humanity of humans, but as far as I'm concerned, it never gets old. I feel happiness at some good or prosperous thing, just as I feel pain at misfortune.

As darkness descended outside and the city's street lamps lit up, some of the regular customers arrived early. They postponed the dancing by ordering something simple to eat in addition to their drinks. It was a way of equipping themselves to enjoy the night from its beginning until the time their bodies reached an absolute limit.

As the numbers increased, so too did their noise and smoke. I also noticed that my father was drinking and smoking more too. Whenever he came over to order another glass, he would say to us, "It's okay, it's okay. One time won't hurt, and tonight is a special night. It deserves the biggest possible celebration."

Instead of reviving my fears and my attempts to explain and judge his behavior, I preferred just to believe him. I said to myself, "I have to learn to accept him as he is, with all his contradictions. For who doesn't contain contradictions? No one! It's not my place to keep imposing, both upon my mind and upon him, the image of him that I want."

As usual, when he saw that the place had filled up, and after the band members had taken their places, he mounted the stage. He took the microphone off its stand and brought it up to his mouth in order to inaugurate the nightly festivities with his multilingual monologue: some humorous, joking passages and some words to warm up the crowd. Every night he adopted a different personality to act out: a taxi driver, a famous singer, a soldier, a chattering woman, a vegetable seller, a soccer player, a doctor, and so on. Rosa got up next to him to translate whenever necessary. Tonight, he was lighter, more cheerful, more joyful, and more into his character than any previous night. I discovered as I watched him up there with the lights pouring over him that my father was extremely handsome, self-confident, and strong. He exuded life.

He began in a purposefully exaggerated tone of voice, saying, "Good evening, ladies and gentlemen! I hope you're having a wonderful evening, O my magnificent people!"

They lit up, as usual, with a surge of claps and whistles, and one of them shouted, "Long live the king!"

The rest repeated it, laughing, "Long live the king! Long live the king!"

After that, he gave a little cough, like someone clearing his throat. He mimed straightening his tie even though he didn't have one, and the crowd laughed. From what he said and his bearing, his facial expressions, and the tone of voice he had assumed up till this point, it seemed that his performance today would facetiously adopt the guise of a king or a political speaker.

"I order you today to loosen the belts around your waists, for we have an endless supply of drinks, and we need the oil to gush from your pockets. Furthermore, I command you to dance until you burst the seams of your underwear. Because tonight I have magnificent news for you: my royal heir, Prince Saleem, will marry Princess Fatima!" Everyone turned toward us with applause, whistling, and congratulations.

"As for Queen Rosa and my own royal highness, we will move to the great country of Germany. My crown prince will remain to take my place. Therefore, I caution that none of you dare annoy him, for in that case I'll come flying, and you know what I'll do to you!"

Someone shouted, "What will you do?"

He responded immediately, "I will invite you to have whatever you want, and I'm paying!"

There was laughter and applause. My father continued his speech, skillfully intimating what he wanted to be taken seriously and what he intended to be humorous. He kept repeating the word "magnificent" frequently.

Next to me, Fatima's cheeks were flushed, and her constant smile was even wider and sweeter tonight. She moved so lightly that she scarcely touched the ground as she filled the customers' orders and replied to their congratulations. I let her know that I was thinking of changing this place's function later on, perhaps from a club to an Arabic restaurant.

"I'm no good at balancing all these contradictions. I couldn't handle managing a club like my father, Fatima."

She agreed with the idea and said that she would cook amazing dishes: "I'll make them line up for couscous in droves."

My father said into the microphone, "I want to thank everyone for their warm hospitality toward us in our exile. I want you to know that the idols in Iraq will certainly fall. I say the idols, and I don't mean the statues. At that time, we'll return to rebuild our beautiful village so that it will be a land for tourists, not for graves. We'll call it Freedmen, or The Absolute, or Dignity. O God, maintain our love for freedom and for human dignity. Kill us as you want or as we want, not as our enemies want. And let the people say 'Amen'!"

The crowd echoed, "A-a-men!"

"And everyone is invited to be our guest! But, well, we won't open a club there, of course."

One of the women called out, "Then what will you open for your guests?"

"I'll open your legs for them!" There was laughter, applause, and whistles.

I let Fatima know that I thought we should bring my Cuban neighbor to work with us in our future restaurant. I also told her that I thought we should take my father's and Rosa's apartment because it had two rooms. "That way, it would be possible for your sister to live with us too. We'll also need it for the children. And we will . . . ."

Fatima put her finger lovingly on my lips, cutting off the flow of what I thought we'd do in the future. I'd been speaking as though guided by my father's words about what was to come. "Shhh," she said. "We'll keep on living, Saleem. We'll keep on living. For now, let's just enjoy this performance."

Three days later, my father handed over his keys to me . . . without the bullet.

Three days after that, my father and Rosa departed for Germany.

After three more days, I learned that the young diplomat had been transferred to the Iraqi embassy in Berlin a week earlier.

Translator's Acknowledgments

Many thanks to Muhsin for entrusting me with his novel and to Khaled al-Masri for guiding my work. Thanks also to Larry Rosenberg and Darlene Leafgren, my first two readers, for their encouragement and support.

Modern Arabic Literature

The American University in Cairo Press is the world's leading publisher of Arabic literature in translation.

For a full list of available titles, please go to:

mal.aucpress.com